Synergy: A Synopsis of an Elite Business Partnership

Nadiya Albishchenko

Vinay Gandhi

Dedication

We would like to dedicate this book in commemoration of the United Arab Emirates Golden Jubilee.

UAE is a land of opportunities not only opening doors for many young entrepreneurs but also supporting growth and investment in the region by leading corporates and businesses from around the world, creating carrier opportunities for the Global communities.

Led by very open-minded, progressive, and determined leaders that have been behind its success and having the slogan "Make it Happen!", the young country has proved itself to stand by its beliefs.

We thank this land that has given us the ground to help us grow our vision and dreams and wish this country everlasting Peace, Love, Prosperity and Success.

Win, Victory, and Love to all!

This book is written with the intention of helping people learn from real-life experiences, not by any means to offend, discriminate, or hurt any person's feelings. We personally thank one and all people in our lives who have helped us to be where we are today, and without them, the journey would not have been the same.

Taking the opportunity, we also thank all our Family, Friends, Well-wishers and everyone that believed in us that has helped us complete this book, and we hope that this will be an inspiration for many.

Last but not least, we thank each other for the trust and faith and for supporting each other through different phases of the book and, in the end, making it Happen!

Table of Contents

Introduction

A business book written by two Successful Business Owners narrates:

Their journey on how they navigated through their businesses to finally come together as Elite Business partners.

Talking about a young entrepreneur who grows up with a dream to start his own business and the challenges and learnings that help him achieve it.

Struggles faced during his journey and his experiences with various business associates through different stages of his business carrier.

Talking in detail about the influences and thoughts towards forming a decisive business partnership.

Dares and obstacles challenged by him during his years of experiences that made him walk on the path toward finding a virtuous business alliance.

This book also talks about a young girl with a desired passion that helped pave her path to establishing a successful business.

How she managed to break through, coming from an orthodox communist background, making the best of every situation, and proving that limitations are just a mindset.

Her experiences with the corporate world and its challenges that made her stronger and wiser over the years.

Struggling through betrayals and perfidies with various business partnerships.

And not only sharing her views and details of what is needed to be a successful Entrepreneur but also her insights on start-ups, build-ups and detailed requirements to help establish a well-synchronized business partnership.

****

Packed with Emotion, Drama, and Lessons learnt from practical experiences.

Full of Encouragement, Positivity, and detailed Learning, not only for budding entrepreneurs but also for experienced business owners and establishments that face day-to-day challenges.

Motivating to help manage a successful business—a must-have inspirational guide for any business venture!

Chapter 1
The First Impression

Have you ever had in your mind what your dream job is? Mine had a simple equation. I just typed on Google search: "The largest company in the world", and the top of the result was where my target was. One day, I wanted to work for the largest corporate structure on the globe. My idea to work there was not only about a stable and good income but also about learning the secrets of a successful business on an international scale.

The Corporate world is not a place for emotions. To climb the business ladder and reach career heights is the main aim, and people are obsessed with it to levels that one cannot imagine. There is just one rule that there are no rules. Yes, on the face of it, all one needs are to be known and follow are the terms of etiquettes, dressing, soft skills, and the way one should talk the business jargons, but a little beneath the skin, it is a jungle and survival of the fittest is the only thing that matters. A ruthless reality that knows no mercy and spares no one, one has only two choices: either to be the hunter or be hunted; master the game and play it right or get played and be the victim.

But I choose to work smartly and keep away from the corporate politics and games. I was just filtering and learning what I thought was the best for me and was honestly giving my best at my job. Young, full of enthusiasm, along with fresh new ideas and big dreams. However, my corporate world experience, to begin with, had a very different approach.

In the mid-way of my corporate employment, I was given an assignment to market a new range of food products. Being a creative thinker, I thought of a few new ideas and planned to introduce new recipes that incorporated food (various chocolates) into beverages and made a unique concept. It sounded a bit crazy at that time, but not for me. …After researching and talking to my own network of professionals, chefs and baristas, I managed to get some buyers interested in my innovative project. I needed to fine-tune it and needed professional help. So, through referrals, I managed to get an appointment with an owner of one of the general trading companies in the region, who also, at that time, had the first and only Barista training institute in the region.

I was quick to take an appointment with him. Reaching his premises, I was totally amazed at the set-up; it was a totally different world, a new world of Independent Businesses. The workplace was a combination of office built within the stores, the owner himself was managing the operations, and anyone could reach out to him at his office without any boundaries, not even a receptionist. Coming from a corporate background where we would need to go through various channels to even meet our own manager/s, this was a thrilling experience: no waiting rooms, no meeting rooms, I could just walk in. Maybe it was my strong personality, or it was just the office culture, but no one asked me anything. I just went towards his office as he seemed to have his own cabin and looked in charge. This being my first experience, I have to admit, it was not as I expected.

A warm smile and a hospitable welcome from him as soon as I knocked at his office door to introduce myself. He was expecting me, of course! He stood up like a gentleman, a tall, presentable, and dynamic personality, smart for sure he had to be, as he had already been running a well-established business since 1999.

I, a young white-collar worker with a background and experience in a glamorous corporate world, walked into the office of someone completely controversial to my idea of a business owner, whose dissimilarity was something that made me fascinated and curious. But, presenting a lunatic idea/concept that most didn't understand, I just hoped it would not give him a weird impression about me.

He took me around the premises, explained the products, and I found some of them were identical to our range. However, their prices were much more competitive. Being a representative of the Principal Company, I could not understand how they could manage to do so. He expressed briefly how they sourced the materials from various global markets to ensure better pricing and assured me that everything in his store was original and imported officially with the required approvals from the authorities of the region. These were the kinds of companies that were always a challenge to any multinational as they competed with them head-on by sourcing materials through the best possible sources, grabbing opportunities, and taking risks without any restrictions or limitations. They bring stocks through different international import channels; keep their overheads in-check compared to the Corporates, making sure to have competitive prices yet make decent margins. Giving the corporation a run-through-the-mill experience, especially in sectors of traditional trade where prices played a major factor. A quite disturbing fact is to see the direct competition of the same product range, but at the same time, my gut was jumping with excitement to learn more about how they operated and managed it against such large corporates.

During the conversation, I discovered that we had common know-how of the market; we followed the same market trends and had a lot of similar opinions about certain concepts. It was not hard to express my new ideas as he seemed to be the man on the ground understanding every phase and stage of the sector. While having a conversation with him on various subjects, he asked me to go see the barista trainer and his partner at his barista training centre. It was so casual and easy; suddenly, lightning struck my head, and my brain started generating millions of ideas on how this could work and create recipes in my mind. If I could manage to break the ice with the help of a professional, this idea would help me promote my brand to new levels which no one had thought of. It could open a window to a whole new world.

My over-enthusiastic self could not help but to share my concept and thoughts with him on how it could work and promote beverage sales and, later, how we could introduce the same concept to star properties, restaurant chains, and cafes in the region. The possibilities seemed endless. He grabbed the idea in an instant, to my astonishment. In fact, he liked the unique, innovative idea and complimented me on doing something out of the ordinary. For the first time, with all my experiences, someone did not reject what I was presenting on the table, and it was also complimented.

He seemed quite keen about it, listening with a lot of interest and understanding the process. We started to bridge the gaps in the concept with his views and ideas that fit into mine, and I could already see my concept shaping up from just a theory. In my mind, there was a major storm filled with better ideas to further develop the concept. His input gave me tremendous encouragement and confidence that I was heading in the right direction with my out-of-the-box idea. At last, someone who got me right away without fancy presentations and endless convincing, someone improvising on the thought process and believing in it straight away, what a relief it was for me. I was not a lunatic with my crazy ideas ☺!

He was the business owner, managing all operations personally; everything was created by him and belonged to him. With no ego, he was open-minded welcoming new ideas and concepts, and he seemed to have a knack for being an innovator himself. An expert communicator with an apprehension of expressing the right expression tactfully for grabbing one's attention. For sure, it was the result of his experience of communicating over the years. The soft timber in his voice suggested confidence, and one could feel optimism throughout the whole conversation. The power and authority of a person who gave me assurance—I can do and do it and do it right!

In my mind, he became the one that I could rely on, share my ideas with, develop them, and put them to try and master them before implementing and launching them into action. So, the next steps were defined for me to be in touch with his Barista Training Centre. I left as an overenthusiastic person with the optimism that some real outcome was expected to happen that would help build a strong alliance between us moving forward.

As for my appointment at the Barista training centre, I was there, but he was not. Perhaps he being there would have made a difference. The visit was not as great as I had expected it to be. In fact, it was frustrating since I found the head trainer, who hosted my visit, to be very negative to my concept. I felt that she was not able to understand and was just into her traditional beverage skills and my unorthodox way of concoction of the beverages she could not accept. Definitely, she had limitations and was very close-minded to anything new, and convincing seemed like a dead end of the road going nowhere.

I did not feel like going back to the owner and expressing my thoughts to him. At the end of the day, he was the one paying her salary to handle the operations and scope of responsibilities as a Barista certified employee. In my opinion, there were much more qualified baristas who would understand the whole concept and help move it to the next level. He did not call me or ask me the feedback about my visit. I thought maybe I was just another drop in the ocean among different lines of businesses that were in his portfolio, and he may not be really fascinated with my project to expedite it further, and everything froze after that meeting. This was not really something that could hold me back from focusing on my concept, so I diverted myself towards other alternatives to give it light.

Almost 5 years later, I understood that our meeting was destined for me to achieve something bigger and better from it; his impression had left a permanent mark in my subconscious; one day, I shall, too, have my own company and be my own boss. All these years, I have not forgotten our first meeting.

I had never felt that spark before. Destiny had its own plan, and we met again, having an opportunity to work together on a newer, bigger project. He was none other than my co-author Vinay Gandhi, the founder and owner of Golden Star International LLC.

Chapter 2
The Inception of Rejuvenation

"Hello, I am Nadiya! We have an appointment…" These are exactly the words I remember when Ms. Nadiya Albishchenko (it took me years to master the spelling) walked directly into my office. I am the kind that believes in an easy approach and likes to be a part of my team always. So, you don't really need to pass through walls to reach me; some of my close business associates come straight into my office as I keep my office door always open and am involved with my team hands-on with their daily operations.

Because of the confidence she wore, no one asked her anything when she reached the door of my office. I took my eyes off my laptop screen to see a tall blonde, grey-eyed, and young female with a wide smile and an energized approach.

Of course, she had an appointment, and I was expecting her; she was right on time, as she has always been. Nadiya was introduced through a common business friend who recommended her to me, describing her as one of the most dynamic, intelligent, and focused ladies from the food trading industry.

Because of my past experience in the industry, I never place my judgment based on others' observations. Owing a Barista training institute, the very first in the region, and the desire to promote it in every possible manner is what interested me to meet Nadiya. Back then, Nadiya was working for a multinational that specialized in commercial instant coffee and was trying to work into the institutional side with new innovative ideas. This is how she was recommended to me, and our meeting was to feel and understand how and if we could work together. I was a hard nut to get fascinated easily, with my years in the industry knowing better than to judge the book by its cover.

But in my opinion, the first impression is always a lasting one. I have to admit my admiration for confidence with the right attitude… However, the proof always lies in the pudding!

"A green tea… Thank you!" Her answer has never changed over the years whenever I've offered her something to drink. After a brief conversation, it was obvious she was a sharp, focused intellectual trying to listen and analyze as we had our conversation; she kept on asking things and possibly was trying to look into how we could work. Being from a traditional business background, I preferred to give her as little information as possible. Then we went to visit our store, and I was amazed by the way she was screening the items. She was inquisitive and curious about how we managed so many SKUs, including a few that her company had failed to get within the region. I was amazed by her sense of alertness, and her point of view was very different from the regular salespeople I meet in the market. Beauty with brains is a lethal combination, and I have to be alert! She kept on asking about my business, how many years I have been in the industry, what I do, how I run the operation, and which sectors I am actively strong in… I felt she was interviewing me… Haha! Knowing myself, I would always go with the flow and tactfully redirect from answering what I didn't want to reveal.

She was offering me a lot of solutions and ideas about Beverages and selling her brand to me, a brand that I had already worked with years ago, even before she was a part of it, but I did not mind associating with it again to help my institute. So, I asked her to visit our Coffee training institute and discuss her plan with our senior trainer. After a little more conversation, she left, and I still remember calling my brother, who is also an active business partner, and kept on describing her with all my enthusiasm. My brother, a man of few words, gave me a smirk, knowing that I am not an easy person to impress.

He told me, "I am sure she is really good, for you to praise her!"

That was our first meeting; I took some feedback from our senior trainer in the institute the next day. Nadiya, as promised, had visited her and saw the place, but to my surprise, she did not give me any feedback about her visit. I supposed she wasn't that keen. Considering that maybe she didn't want to say it directly to me and presuming she was just being courteous towards the approach, I did not pursue it too. However, she managed to leave a lasting impression on me through her strong personality and her intellectual, out-of-box thinking.

Chapter 3
At the Beginning

Life goes on, and so did my business! A business that I had started in 1999 in a small manner exporting split units, television sets, water heaters, garments and anything and everything I could get my hands on to the Subcontinent and Africa except for foodstuff. Basically, I wanted to do business, but working for a food trading company, I wanted to be honest with my profession and the company, leaving the fact alone that the company I was working for belonged to my uncle, whom I looked up to as a shrewd, successful businessman. The business has been something I always felt I was born to do; I was happy while making some additional income on the side to help support my lifestyle and family.

My uncle's company was a great business school for me; I basically learnt a lot there…a lot of what I should and much more of what I shouldn't do. You see, I believe all bosses are teachers; some teach what you *need to do* and a few that teach what you *should not*. It is to our capabilities and capacity to take it, modify it, tweak it to our understanding, filter it and grasp what we need from it. I always say there is one teacher explaining the same thing to thirty students in the class, but only a few score straight As' while a few others struggle even to pass. So, it is not always the capacity of the teacher, but a lot also depends on the capacity of the student's eagerness to learn. My uncle is an intense businessman, a person, fearless and bold when it comes to business. His shrewdness and the appetite to take risks is a gift that still amazes me. He meant business, be it even with his own blood and family, so hardcore determined and focused that there was no place for emotions—an 'all men for themselves with the last-man-standing attitude'. He believed that if you have the perks, people will take the shit that you throw at them…I agree to a large extent! He was a practical thinker and an amazing businessman but a little too cold and extreme, to my understanding, then. Nevertheless, it was a business school for me, a school that taught me a lot about what I should not be and something about how I should be. I believe business is in the gut of a person; not all are blessed with it.

Well, part of the reason I felt my uncle to be a little extreme was my father. My father was a businessman, too, not a successful one, though. I still remember his electrical shop in the neighbourhood, my first real business world, where I used to go and spend most of my evenings after school. Hardly 12 years of age, I was so passionate about the shop. At school, all I could think of was to go home, change, grab a snack, and rush to the shop, which was the thing that inspired me to get up in the morning. I could leave playing football or cycling around the neighbourhood as all I cared about was to reach home and rush to my papa's shop. Well, my papa was a contrast to my uncle. He was a soft, caring, careless, giving kind of a businessman, someone who had no place in the business world. He would be shy to ask for his deserved job charges, felt sorry for his clients if they would give excuses and pardoned their payments based on nothing but just words and excuses. He trusted their conditions and was extremely flexible all the time. And people knew it and used to take advantage of his sentiments. He could not last long, he tried several times, but he lacked any and all signs of a true Businessperson. He had dreams…he had the attitude of a great business owner but never the mind or heart of one.

One can act and believe in being a great achiever, but a great achiever does not act to be one; they just are achievers, and that's just how it is.

My papa was soft to everyone, even to people he hardly knew and met for the first time; customers used to use his services and not pay him, buy goods from him and pay him half the price. I used to get annoyed by his manner of working. Even though I was just 12 years old, I knew this is not how a business runs; this is not how one manages a business. My frustration was obvious to many of his customers, who I already knew were using him for their own benefit as I was always spending all my spare time at his shop. I still remember fighting with one of his clients while they just smiled at a 12-year-old kid. They went and complained about me to my father, that I had no manners to talk. Not to my surprise, he got mad at me and told me that a business is run on a relationship and not just with money, and my argument was: what is the use of having a business if all you needed was relationship and respect? You can have good relationships working a nine-to-five job. He hated my guts; he always had. I was the black sheep in the family, always a rebel, always challenging the way things were, be it his way of handling the business or handling the family. His manner of working and work ethic always left us in a state of poverty, as he would always lose money due to his flimsy business policies and approaches.

Possibly, when I started to work for my uncle and saw his attitude towards business was purely commercial and not for building relationships, it got me very fascinated in a manner a voice inside told me I was right when I used to fight with my papa. It kind of helped me to justify my feelings with my papa and his theory that always suppressed me within myself. It did not take me much time to understand that a business neither runs 100% on money nor 100% on relationships. A business is a balance between money and relationships, but the beauty is to balance them to a point where it benefits you; it's all about negotiating, convincing in the end, about winning and making something from it. It was just business at the end of the day, and as long as one could balance the relationship and the economics of it without dropping either end, it was the key to the success of a reliable and sustainable business model.

This is something that I was taught by someone whom I consider played a vital role in teaching me a lot of business lessons, someone who inspired and influenced me, my first business Guru—my mom, an ordinary housewife who was not allowed to sprout in the cruel world of a Man-dominated society, my very first Boss from birth!

Chapter 4
Do Not Stop Believing in Yourself

My mother, my first mentor, way of explanation is mostly through the usage of parables that she would quote and allow us to understand and see things through our own parameters and gauge life to our best capacity. Some of her favourites were: "Wear what the world likes to see you in, but eat what you like." If you try to understand this, it has a very deep meaning to it asking us to behave as per the ethical manner of the world but to live as we desire. Another meaning is to keep your mind civilized and let your heart be wild, and another meaning would be to listen to the world, be thankful, and do what you feel is right; no one else is in your place, and you and only you alone can decide for yourself. I can go on but rather leave it to you readers to think over it than me vocalizing my thoughts to you.

Another very deep parable she used was, "No one can bear to see a happy person nor spare a dime for a needy one," which is so true. People don't like to see others happy or successful; they compare themselves to them, feeling jealous and envious of a successful person once they know they have made/reached a point of success. They start thinking why, why not them, accusing, reasoning that the success was just luck or it happened because of help from someone or accusing that they must have done it in an inappropriate manner to achieve success in life… I have hardly heard someone say, "Wow!' The person deserves it for the hard work that has gone into it! And at the same time, if a day comes when one comes across a friend or a relative in need, they find every excuse to show how they would like to help but cannot, and all friends and relatives suddenly disappear.

My mom is an only child to her parents, and in a male-dominated society, I have no doubt about how tough she became over the years. Growing up under her strong determination and focus helped me program myself to a great extent being bullheaded towards my target.

Mummy was robust yet very subtle; she taught me a lot about different ways to look at things, and patience was beyond expression (I am still trying to master that). Calm, quiet, focused…one could rarely see the tension on her face. She was always under tremendous pressure and struggling with life's challenges but always had a smile on her face. With all her limitations, she still managed much more than expected. Being a popular private tutor in the neighbourhood, she used to have a good number of children coming home for extra lessons. She had a reputation for being a good institution teacher, and students used to understand her way of explanation and performed better academically.

<u>"Life is a crude lesson—the kind one can't graduate without multiple failures; unless you master it, it keeps on coming back at you!"</u>

If you are open to learning from Life, it keeps on teaching you endlessly. What Life has taught me is that <u>no one can master life</u>; just go with the flow, keep learning, and keep improving. This is the only way to go with it; it is, and it has always been a blessing if you find genuine acquaintance/s who actually feel happy for you and someone who will stand with you to help you without purpose, not because they feel great helping or feel sorry for you but just because they care and want to do it for you without expecting anything in return, not even a thank you! Mostly, everyone has a motto behind all their actions, if nothing else, a self-satisfying ego that I helped someone and the feeling of self-greatness doing so.

Over the years, it has become harder for me to accept any kind of favours. I prefer people telling me, "I want to help you because you helped me", or "I help you because I feel great after that". In a way, I have noticed that not only I but even my siblings help subconsciously because they want to and not because they expect anything in return; I feel it is purely the influence of my mother's nature on all of us.

I feel that the kind of parables she used are the kind that can only be chosen by a person who has lived and learnt life through one's own meandering experiences, she has many more, and I can probably write them in a separate book altogether.

Today, I feel she has gone beyond her own teaching when there are times I remind her about her quotes, and she smiles with agreement. I think, compared to when she was younger, she has learnt from her struggles to not take life too utterly anymore. This is something I still need to learn; one can't be taught everything; something is just meant to be experienced to understand!

I feel proud to admit that I have always been my mama's boy. No matter how challenging it has got for her to manage me…I probably was the only one who was blessed with the power to test her patience. Right from my childhood, I have always been a very inquisitive and curious child, jumping into any kind of adventure, getting into a lot of trouble, and trying everything I was told not to just to see what happens. This nature of behaviour has played an important role in me to take any challenge boldly. But as a child, this kind of adventurous nature would drag any guardian into insanity, especially if they cannot relate to it, but even though it may have been a challenge for someone like her to manage me at times, this nature of mine being curious helped me a lot to explore in life, learn and experience many phases of life which I could have never in a shell of trying to prove to be an obedient child.

The best part of it is that this attitude has taught me to know myself better, and I do admit to consciously taking chances with life over the years right from my childhood, some very bold challenges. I also know at times, it got hard for her to manage me, but I adored the fact she could keep her calm beyond my expectation if I have to compare myself to her even today.

At times, she could understand that I could not help being me. What I learnt from her was to let go of many things, forgive and forget something that is always hard to do. Let us just say that I kind of took great advantage of it, but no matter what, I always liked to be in her company, learn, observe, challenge, and also oppose her in a lot of ways. Be it good or bad, these challenges made me learn more about the times, people, and the world, giving me endless insight into life itself!

Having said this, I grew to understand her more. As I was growing, I started to be more caring towards her, helping her with small chores in the house and surprising her with a cup of tea on a lazy Friday afternoon. These were some small gestures I performed to show my gratitude to her for being my role model in life.

It is true my mom is an iconic figure of my childhood, someone I would always look up to, someone whom I know has added value to my being. Besides many, she also taught me not to wait to be taught by life but to go figure it out. The purpose of life is not to follow the rules but to get it done and get the results. A classic example is her limited to no exposure to the work culture; her skill set of grasping things and figuring things out was beyond explanation. I can still picture her doing accounts for my father's company, and I could see her calm and composed self, trying to understand while my not-so-patient papa kept expressing and panicking about bookkeeping entries. With her grace, she could hold on, understand, and actually figure out the entries that needed to be passed in the book of accounts. I am no auditor to audit her, but what amazed me was her skill set and the fact she managed to figure it out to help my papa do his book with basic account entries. This helped me learn that it is not the way you do things that matter but the inclination to do it that counts. Once you are determined to do it, you will find a way and figure it out. With the right attitude, one can always manage to do it and do it right!

It was great to see them work together at times. I would observe how long it would last, and trust me, I don't know of anyone else in my life who could ever handle my papa's over-reactive and, in a lot of ways, impatient nature. I guess my DNA got the potency from him, and now, when I think about it, I feel she could manage her serenity with me due to the practice she had with my papa. My curiosities, impatience, and inquisitiveness were possibly inherited from my papa, combined with my mother's influence; my grooming as a child helped me get through a lot in life and in business. She is my first mentor, in many ways, my business Guru. I often commented to her that she had the quality of a successful entrepreneur and she should start a business of her own. To date, she just laughs it out, but in the laugh, one can feel she knows I was right, and what I feel is that due to her limitations, she somehow used me as an outlet for pouring her skill sets, nurturing the entrepreneurship in me.

She has a simple *funda* in life: "Whatever happens, happens for the best!" With this in her mind, nothing has ever shaken her up. A strong personality, an amazing mentor, and a priceless blessing she has been. I have seen her go through some of the most devastating times with a smile on her face, contributing a lot in my life to help me take life by its horn and making me the fighter I am today. With all that she had in her, what was even more amazing was the trust she had in me, her faith in my capabilities that one day I shall make it in life …which possibly I could not see in me at that time, but she somehow had a clear vision which helped me take some drastic steps later in life.

When I first started my own small trading business, she was the sole person who stood with me. I spoke to her, stating that I wanted to start something and step out of my comfort zone; I wanted to be self-employed. I had discussed this with some of my close friends, who thought I was out of my mind, but when I spoke to her, she never discouraged me as if she already knew I could do it! She calmly told me to follow my instincts, quoting her favourite lines, "Whatever shall happen, shall happen for the best!"

When I took my first step towards going into my very own business, she was the one who stood with me, believed in me, and even dared me at a point. It was a few weeks into my new business, and I lost almost thirty percent of my investment (my hard-earned savings), and when I told her about it, I could not believe what she said. She told me, "Now you know better, and you still have seventy percent of the money left with you." A big smile followed, and my eyes shined like the Sirius star on a new moon night. This statement shook me up; even to this day, it gives me goosebumps when I speak about it. These ordinary words from what the world saw as an ordinary homemaker were like music to my ears. Those were the words that helped me take my next step towards a fresh start-up giving me back my confidence and encouraging me to move forward and try again to start on my own.

She taught me never to stop believing in my own self:
Thank you, Mummy!!

Chapter 5
My Trading Business

My papa's small electrical shop was on a far corner of Al Musallah Street in the old town of Bur Dubai. I would consider that as my very first business; the way it inspired me and the way it excited me to go to help him after school. I was so excited to finish school and head back home, not to be free to cycle or play football with my friends but to change, have a quick snack prepared by mummy, and rush straight to the shop. I felt at that moment that I had found what I wanted to do in my life…I wanted to manage my own business.

Papa allowed me to sit on his chair when he would be repairing something or would go out of the shop, which he did very often as most of his jobs were on-site. Sitting on that chair gave me a feeling of control, a power that can't be expressed through words. That shop didn't last long due to complications. Plus, my father's softhearted attitude and his blind trust towards people never helped him sustain any business for too long anyway. He was a very hardworking and sincere man. I have seen him work twelve to eighteen hours a day with just short tea and cigarette breaks in between, which helped me understand that if a person is passionate about what they are doing, then a clock is just a piece of art hanging on the wall. But what I also learnt from him was that working hard is never enough if you don't work smart.

However, it's all easier said than done! I could feel the difference when I came to a position to take the leap and jump start my very own business that I did with some small savings that my mother had kept for me. Starting my very own trading business, a company from scratch, gave me a kind of euphoria and made me feel way more special than the way I felt sitting on my papa's chair. Even though sitting in my papa's shop at a very young age made me feel great yet having my own business was incomparable and made me feel unbreakable, strong, and unbeatable. The feeling lasted just for a couple of days…I really wish that it were true and that easy to do your own start-up, but to be frank—**NO!** The only part that is true is the *euphoriasum*, the joy, the thrill, the kick, the high…that I got, which I feel most people get in the beginning.

My first self-owned business was full of challenges. The truth is that I was doing something that did not relate to the industry I was familiar with, as I was already working for my uncle's company and didn't want to do something that would compete, offend or make me feel treacherous towards my duties. It was easier to do that, as managing business that you are familiar with is always easier than working with something new from scratch which you are not well versed with. However, I chose to do that due to my family's respect and relationship. This made it even harder for me to figure things out. I was not sure what I was doing, except for the fact that I was very comfortable working for my uncle, but I needed to come out of it and required to start something on my own at the same time, stay sincere to my uncle and towards my duties. I had never lost my passion or inclination to do my business, but over the years of working for him, I got into a comfort zone. A comfort zone that hallucinated me to believe that I had achieved my goals. In reality, this was not true. I was making money, a lot of it, but not for me, working from 8 am to 9 pm, or at times even later. Handling various divisions of the business, be it logistics, exports, or trading. I used to involve myself everywhere because I was so much driven by the business and wanted to master it.

One should remember that the comfort zone is not always about being lazy or scared to take chances. In my case, it was different. With experience, I realized if one has the passion and the inclination to grow and learn and a stage/platform is provided for them to do so, the person tends not to care about anything else and continues working even if it does not provide the growth or benefit for their own personal self. One uses such opportunities to keep working, hypnotized with an impression that they are growing towards their goals without realizing that all the pain and hard work is not for their own achievements but for someone else.

This is a much more dangerous comfort zone, as a person tends to be blinded by their passion and gets exploited by others at the stake of their own desire. This kind of comfort zone tends to blur one's far-sighted vision, and one feels achieving short goals for others is the only purpose, tends to forget about their own objectives being too engrossed with their thirst to learn, they keep enjoying what they are doing continuously putting their energies into it.

Working for my uncle, I did the same. I have always been a hardcore salesperson, always switched on, ready for potential business…all this because I am passionate about what I do and how I do it. I have always admired and adored my challenging self. It was not about being benefited, but what was more important for me was that I was enjoying what I was doing, and I knew that I was good at it. It had never been about being lazy or sluggish; my comfort zone was more about me being so much engulfed by my routine that it never crossed my mind to come off it. When you are allowed to work with your own passion, and you feel the comfort of doing so, it is then that the very thought of change never crosses your mind.

I was confident, energetic, connected…enjoying making money…although not for myself. The fact that I was doing it so successfully gave me a feeling of tranquility. It's truly one's passion that can put one in a comfort zone to a level that one does not care if they are exploited to benefit others, as long as one manages to use one's desire to satisfy one's hunger. I had reached a point where I didn't bother with who was benefiting from my work as long as I was enjoying what I was doing and was getting a thrill from it.

What I've learnt is: If you work with passion, the appreciation or encouragement of others is not what is important, but what really kicks in is a kind of satisfaction; it is like a release of dopamine in your brain; you are so drugged that you are not interested in anything else but that taste and the satisfaction of achieving and getting your job done. I still remember the days when I would work until late, yet on my way home, I would have a smile of achievement on my face because I managed to get the job done. I didn't care how someone was taking advantage of my skills and benefiting from them as long as I was getting a thrill from them. This was my comfort zone, giving my complete sincerity to what I was doing. I guess all passionate people are like performers on the stage of life, not doing it to be awarded but just giving their best performance every time, bettering themselves not for the world but just to prove to themselves that they are better today than yesterday, an applaud would be the best gift. This went on for over five years, with false promises of growth from my uncle, which used to brighten some of my days exceptionally. I guess it was like applause for me, and I kept getting more and more into the business. But, like everything has an end, so did my ignorance, and upon realizing it, it was time for me to come out of my comfort zone.

It all happened when a moment came in my life when I met some old schoolmates and started hanging out with them. I realized they were doing so good for themselves, financially way better than me. They looked upon me as a mentor, took my advice and guidance, and respected me for what I had achieved. I even managed to place them in some of the reputed companies and learnt they were hired just on my recommendation and were offered more than what I was drawing; they were thanking me and giving me the credibility to help them grow in their careers… I was happy for them, but it made me realize and question myself, where was I? The clear answer was I was not growing. Don't get me wrong, I was growing within myself with my skills and knowledge, perhaps just being happy about it, but the fact that I was not growing economically made me feel brutally exploited, used, and betrayed. This was when I decided to start something on my own. I knew If I could do it for someone else, I could definitely do it for myself.

Easy to say, though. I was so much into what I was doing that somewhere in my head, I didn't want to let that go, but a little deeper within me, my heart already clearly indicated that it was a thankless journey of ungratefulness and selfishness where I would keep making my employer richer and richer and he would just sit back and keep enjoying it, giving me a minuscule growth and depriving me of what I truly deserve. Don't get me wrong, I don't blame him; it was me who allowed it to happen. I allowed myself to be exploited. I did speak to my boss-uncle openly on the fact that he should consider my growth and that I already had too much on my plate, yet I was willing to take on more responsibility, but I needed to grow along, to which he promised me a lot of things such as creating a separate division for me, giving me a small share in that division, moving me to another regional office, and…I believed him, and it dragged on for another two years until I finally understood it would never happen. I needed to break out of my comfort zone; it was clear that the only person who could help me was me.

I am thankful to him, my friends, and everyone that I took encouragement from to come out of my happiness zone (comfort zone) and make it happen…a decision I shall never regret!

The company I initiated to start was by myself, my own, without any business associates or partners…just a step too bold to be taken without any backup or support. Stepping into the business was not easy, as I was not even sure what I would do with it. The business was as a general trader in the outskirts of Dubai, a little less developed emirate to help me do it with the least expense as I had very little savings thanks to my Mom's saving mentality. During the first few weeks in the business and K-boom…I lost almost thirty percent of my funds. It was not a business deal, nor was it my mistake; it was a pure act of being cheated, welcome to the real world! You see, UAE, home to some of the most modern societies with a sense of tolerance and acceptance, back then had a primitive manner towards work; they required a UAE national to be a fifty-one percent stakeholder in the company during those days (now, of course, you have options) and the sleeping partner I managed to start the company with just vanished with the money that I gave him to get some initial paperwork done based purely on trust. This is where I got disappointed. The first couple of months in business, and I already wanted to call it quits as I was scared to lose the rest of the little savings I had. Thanks to the encouragement from my mother, I had the inclination to continue. And thus began the new change in my life, and I finally decided that I shall continue to take my chances until I succeeded.

Chapter 6
Giving Up Is Not in the Options

Me, talking to myself… I have what it takes; If I can do it for someone else, why not for myself? I am great, I have the power…but in reality, these are just words that one uses if they are not sure about themselves. All inspirations, thoughts, and speeches are for people to remind them what they are. I was soon to realize that I didn't need those reminders; all I needed was to understand how I shall work for my dream company. The only network I had was with people I knew from the Industry I had been working with and to keep my professional ethics. I chose not to cross lines with my uncle's company. Hence, I opted not to work with the same industry, I was tempted numerous times to do so, but I did not want to go beyond my self-acceptance with the company I had been with for over six years, plus the family ties that I needed to respect. This made it the most challenging moment of my life. What would I really do?

Then I got an opportunity: I had a close friend whose father was working for the garment industry and had a lot of shirts, tops, and towels that were not getting sold or had less demand sitting in the factory occupying space. My friend discussed this with me and told me she could speak to her father and get these items for me at a fraction of the cost, the factory just wanted to liquidate the stocks as demands were low, and they didn't have space while they were busy preparing new orders. The next thing I knew; I was already at the place checking it out. The deal was: I would pay them once I sold the goods. They were happy I opted to fill my old Cressida station wagon full of boxes from their store; I was so confident I could sell it. Based on trust, my friend's father agreed to allow me to do so. Also, generously guided me where I could possibly offer the products and expressed to not sell them in the markets where they were already present. But that was not my plan.

I had a client who was buying a lot of items from the company I was working for to take to Africa, and she had a general store where she sold so many other generic things besides basic edible commodities that she was buying from me. She was in town along with her brother, who was managing the general department store division for her. It was a great opportunity for me. I called her and told her I had things that would interest her brother, the garments that I was trading privately through my own company.

We shared a very strong business relationship, and she had always told me that I had a knack for doing my own business, and one day, I would. She invited me to her hotel apartment, asking me to bring samples of the items with me. I still remember that instead of taking samples in her room to show her, I asked the concierge to help me take all the boxes up to the room. I was so excited, and I already knew in my heart that I could convince them to buy. You have to believe in your own skill first, and only then can you sell; this is something I have always had in me.

I still remember the look on her face when she saw so many boxes being delivered to her place. She asked me what this was, and I smiled and replied, "All these are boxes belonging to you."

She was a genuine, strong businesswoman and had a liking for my trade skills. It took me nearly an hour to talk to her brother, showing him things and shortlisting things that he approved of. Segregating the wants, maybes, and don't wants...she kept watching me and got involved a few times as she already could feel myself selling all of it to her brother, which she expressed it openly. Well, that was my idea right from the start, anyway ☺.

So, after we had segregated the stocks and he agreed to buy, I asked her brother what he thought of the lot that was segregated as maybes… What if I gave it to him at a thirty percent discount?

To which he replied, "Fifty percent discount."

I was quick to respond, "If all stocks from the maybe collection, yes!"

His sister got shocked, and they started speaking in Swahili, where I could only guess the argument between them. She made sure he would say no.

So, I made a new offer: "Take it for 50 percent, but you also take the stocks that you said you don't want, I shall give it to you at a 70% discount."

Her brother said, "Give me fifty percent price for the maybes and he will pay only twenty percent price for the don'ts," and even before they could discuss, I shook hands and sold all the stocks to them. It was a sweet deal for them and a sweeter one for me.

As I was leaving the hotel apartment, my client looked at my face with a kind of look as if she had just woken up to realize I had actually sold everything to them. She was an amazing person; she appreciated my talent and told me she wished the best for me in my new business…also complimented me that she would send her son to me for training…to which I replied that I would train him for free with a big smile back! ☺

This was the deal that helped me cover my previous losses, gain some added profits, and, above all, it gave me encouragement, helping me get my total confidence back that I was a born salesman. I was blessed with a convincing tongue, and I was never shy of using it.

When I paid a small part of the earnings to my friend, to my astonishment, she told me that she knew I would do it, and she had no doubt about it. Her father could not believe I sold all the stocks. By the way, if you are interested to know—my client from Africa managed to sell most of the stocks they bought from me at a decent margin. This made me really happy! I always sell to my customers with high spirits and with positivity.

Over a period, I have learnt that **the energy and the attitude of the salesperson always matter**. This kind of energy generates a positive vibe that passes on. I believe in it strongly, and to my clients, I always sell with that attitude which somehow helps them to be able to sell better. It has always been my mantra and an important part of the belief I have in myself. Even today, I tell my team to smile over the phone as if the customers on the other side can see it. Be positive and shift your energy to your clients, and they will benefit from doing business with us, which will help them grow and eventually help us expand too.

This deal opened many doors for me, as I realized I already had connections, and these connections were not only buying items from the company I was so honestly working for, but they were also buying other things that were not related to the company, and I could trade with them for those items privately through my company. I started interacting with potential buyers, asking them for their requirements for other items they procured and would be interested to buy from Dubai. To my surprise, I saw a whole network of people working for me. People started sending me requirements for air conditioners, television sets, linen, and foam mattresses, and I started to get involved with a lot of trading activities, however, keeping my core and still working my ass off for the company that gave me a fixed monthly income with minuscule growth. Over a short period, I understood I had more potential to do something by myself and my attention slowly got diverted towards my new development.

I spoke to my elder brother, who was at the moment also similarly struggling to come up in his career; he had good experience in exporting shipments, documentation, and other such stuff, plus the trust which I could always fall back on. His income was even lesser than mine. I had to ask him to quit his job and join me for business, which he readily did without an ounce of doubt. He always believed and still does that I have the brain for it, and he has the muscle to do it! With him joining my team, I had more confidence to move aggressively towards growing my business. In a couple of months, we were, though erratically but sincerely, growing our business. What troubled me was that I could not reach a point of a permanent, stable business. This was a bother for me as I could not run a business that was not consistent. It was time, and I planned to quit my job and join full-time to do my business.

But who would explain this to my uncle? Who would bell the cat? He was and is shrewd, witty, and egocentric…having an ability to read minds was also one of his superpowers, and it was not hard for him to read me too. And letting me go would mean a kind of insecurity for him, even though my intentions were not to have competition nor to have any family conflicts but just to move out peacefully, but I knew if he knew I had a trading business, he would not trust me with my intentions and think I will start competing him. But someone had to do it…and it was only me who had to bell this ferocious cat. I needed to gather a lot of strength to do it, as this was more intense due to the family ties we shared. So, I had to think of a way where I would not offend him. I felt a little alone on this path of life, as it was something I needed to do, and I had no one to guide me. It was just me by myself.

During that period, India, Gujarat, was hit by the 7.7 magnitude Bhuj Earthquake and the whole state was shaken. It was a disaster with a lot of losses of lives. Businesses had shut down across the state; it was among the worst period for any state to be in, and my close school buddy, who had moved back to India with his parents and siblings, was no special. He had lost everything under the quake. I called him to check on him and still remember him crying, stating he had lost everything. He was in the signage business, creating signboards, pasting advertising on vehicles, and many more. I genuinely wanted to help him, and a thought came to call him back to Dubai and start a small signage business with him. This would give me a chance to speak to my uncle and explain to him that I was getting into the advertising business, and, to be frank, I didn't mind the diversification too.

Chapter 7
Well, I Have My Own Plans for the Future

I planned to call my friend and offered him to be my partner to help start an advertising firm here in Dubai. He jumped at the opportunity, and the next thing I knew, we were having a beer at our *aada* (a place where we regularly met to grab a drink), catching up on old times. My friend had grown up in Dubai, and we had gone to secondary and high school together. Over the years, we had become the best of pals, but due to circumstances beyond his control, he had to permanently leave the country. His father already had an established signage company business in the region that they were forced to wind up. I took my chances by asking him to join me in setting up my very first advertising company, hoping to have a stable and constant business which at that stage was my priority, plus this company would be a friendly escape route from my uncle's company.

We were quick to set the business up, and all were super excited to do so. With the help of my brother, who was now well-versed in the documentation and the requirements to set up a new business, the process was quick. What also thrilled him was that this would pave the road for me to join the trading business, which, he believed, if I did, would grow in leaps and bounds. Plus, the excitement of starting a new advertising business was giving all of us another level of inebriation.

My friend was grateful for the opportunity, provided I had made sure he was at his comfort and focused. It did not take time for us to get started, but to keep expense of the licensing for the company low, we opted for the company to start on sole proprietor ownership instead of a private limited company, as it was my investment I opted for my brother to become the sole owner of the company in all righteousness. However, to help my friend feel comfortable, in all fairness, I made him a joint signatory with the bank account. Not that he did not trust me; it was just something I felt would be the right thing to do.

After completing all legalities and formalities to start an advertising company, we were up and running in no time. It was time to canvas for the new business, asking my friend to contact all his previous clients, get into refreshing his networks and start meeting people to revive relationships. Two weeks in the business, and that is all it took for me to understand selling was not his forte; he was just not made for it. He was extremely talented, having steel-steady hands with total precision; seeing him work was amazing. He could run a blade through a straight line with an accuracy of a cutting machine without using a scale; his skills were mind-boggling, but what was even more baffling was his sales skills were equally opposite. He lacked confidence and had no clue how to pitch. After attending a few meetings with him, I came to know that he had this very unique manner of communicating with so many details that complicated things.

Just imagine a surgeon explaining to you the complete process of the surgery that he is going to perform on you, but not in layman's language how he would cut you apart and then stitch you back up, explaining in detail everything he shall do, right from the start of the surgery until the end. That would freak anyone out of their minds, and no one would ever opt for surgery, resulting in the surgeon running out of his business in no time. In this case, my friend would keep explaining the process, how things would happen, and if there was an issue, how he would correct it…all this was not relevant to the client. What they wanted to hear was, "We are at your service, and the job will be done with a guarantee of your total satisfaction." Great! Now I had in my hands two businesses, both with an amazing workforce backing me up but with no one to lead the sales and create the network.

I have had food at celebrity chef restaurants that didn't taste all that great, but the presentation was so amazing that one would grow an appetite for it just by the way it was served, and I have experienced having some amazing food made by chef nobody, and he remained a nobody as he never had what it took to be that somebody. If the food comes on the plate so ordinary, one has to dig into it before experiencing and realizing that it is tasty. Sales is a skill where you have to make people look forward to buying; creating demand is an art. Presenting, convincing, and selling a talent, and **I always say a good salesperson never sells a product; they sell themselves. They are the presentation that would grow the appetite of the buyer.** Their skills, their passions, and their vibes all synchronize to work together and to do so, they have a way of making themselves believe in the product first, and that makes it easier for them to persuade others and make it happen, helping them to close a deal and make the sale. A convincing salesperson is like a surgeon you would put your total trust into.

My experience and exposure in the advertising industry were nil, but my practices over the period had given me the skill to sell, that is what I do, and that is what I do best! So, even though I was in a state of huge disappointment seeing my friend's selling skills yet, to my surprise, I did not panic as I knew I had the best hands for the job, and all I had to do was get him the sales order this was and has always been my strength. Now, the only thing that concerned me was that I had created a point where I had no choice but to take the jump. I had to quit my present job and get serious about taking care of my companies. It reminded me of the quote from Franz Kafka, where he stated, "Beyond a certain point there is no return. This point has to be reached!" I had reached that point of no return, and the only way was to move forward.

So finally, it was time for me to get involved with my businesses. Still working full-time at my present job hardly provided me time to help develop my own businesses, which now I felt more confident about than ever before. It was time for me to face my uncle, my boss, the ferocious cat—yes! I still felt like a little mouse when it came to facing him; it could be the respect, the admiration, the appreciation…or it could just have been the fear created in me over the years working for him. Whatever it was, it needed to be faced and faced by me alone!

Handing a resignation letter was not what I felt to be appropriate, as it was direct family, so I asked him if I could come home to see him in the evening. He agreed to it. I opted to go alone without asking my parents to come along as I did not want to get them involved in my work but to my surprise, even though he saw me alone, he asked me in front of his whole family what I wanted to talk about. I felt very awkward as his wife (my aunt), my cousins, my grandmother, and his elder sister, who were living with him, were around. Possibly you get the picture of why it made me so nervous to talk to him. He was like 'The Godfather' of our family, surrounded by the flock that blindly followed him, and suddenly, I was the rat of the family. No one could go against him. My cousin brother, who was fresh in the company after graduating from an overseas university, knowing their father, felt it might not be a good atmosphere to hang around, so he, with my cousin sister, quietly escaped from the room. It would have made no difference, as I stated earlier, I was already at a point where I had to move forward, and there was no return.

The minute I started to explain to him that I was going to partner with my friend's advertising company and wanted to quit working for him, he snapped and started by saying he had already felt it and had told everyone in the room that I was coming to speak about quitting the job like I said he has this power to read people's mind. He continued speaking about how great he had been by giving me an opportunity, what he had done for my parents, and how he had played God to the family. And no one in that room spoke a word. My father, who failed many times in business, was also working at his company, and he took that as a big favour he had done to us and to me. Nothing that night actually surprised or in any way astonished me. I was already anticipating the reaction and knew the atmosphere was not going to be favourable.

While he went on, I had a moment. Looking at him, he suddenly didn't look that tough to me; the flock was his cover, possibly, and he could not face me alone. Or maybe just wanted to prove a point to himself. His nervousness, anger, and anxiety made him look a little feeble. I had such an episode with him on a personal matter in the past and had seen him do this to other people too, so in a way, his overreaction didn't come as a surprise. I was familiar with his wrath, especially if something was not to his liking or favour or he felt something was going against him. He went on for over forty minutes, and suddenly, all I could see was a man, my role model at a point in life, whose image had just been tarnished within seconds due to this overreaction. I just kept quiet, but a tri-zillion thoughts were going through my mind.

Don't get me wrong, I still have great regard for him; he has been someone who has played a vital role in my life. With and from him, I have learnt a lot, but when I walked out of the house that day, no one, not even my Grandma, had the courage to cool him down. I don't blame her as the whole atmosphere was so unpleasant, but deep down, I had this burst of happiness, the feeling of freedom—I had spoken to the _Don Vito Corleone_ of my family, and I came out alive, and that was how it felt walking out of his house that night.

My brother asked me how it went; I told him very casually that my uncle asked me to give him an official resignation letter tomorrow in the office. My mother, who knew that I was going to talk to him, knowing his nature, asked me how it went, and all I said was he was very upset and asked me to give him an official letter tomorrow. I was so casual after that incident I came out stronger and didn't feel the need to express anything; I was not hurt by his words, I was not upset, I was feeling free, feeling happy, and I felt a kind of strength that was suppressed within me coming out—I was really happy, happy that it went the way it did. If he had been nice and had asked me the reason why I had to go, again promising me a promotion, dragging me another couple of years, that would have been worst, and I would have never had the strength to reject his request due to the respect I held for that man in my heart.

I resigned the very next day as I did not want him to change his mind. This made him very annoyed as I mentioned a notice period of thirty days on my resignation. He took this very personally and ensured that he would use all his power to avenge me. He cancelled my visa with a six-month no-entry into the country. The United Arab Emirates was a growing economy, and as a young market in those days, they wanted to protect entrepreneurs and help them to be successful and to protect the employers in the country. They gave them a lot of powers: one of them was banning entry for employees if they resigned, to insure the employee does not join competition. This ban usually was for six months, and it was commonly practiced by the business owners to protect themselves from competition in the market. This practice was used by the employer to exploit and, in certain cases, threaten their employees. I requested him not to put a six-month-no-entry stamp on my passport as I was not going to be a competitor, and he did it anyway and even explained his act with two lame reasons. One, that if he did not, others will resign tomorrow and request him the same, and two, he wants to keep the policy of the company unchanged. But I knew the true reason; it was that I had the nerve to submit my resignation letter and give him a notice period, and he had to show me who had the last laugh.

Even though he had the capacity to read minds, he missed seeing my capabilities of knowing that. He was very predictable to me, and I had already anticipated this from him. I was prepared for it. I had surreptitiously completed my graduation degree through a correspondence college, giving my exams every two years when I went on my formal vacation to India. All I needed was to get my certificates attested so they would be officially recognized in the UAE, which I did. Again, UAE has always been a place to respect educated people, and the attested graduation certificate would exempt me from the ban of re-entering the country. It took me two weeks to finish my formalities of authenticating my certificates to finally come back to the country of opportunities, officially getting my six-month-no-entry-stamp void.

Now, more than ever, I had no obligations whatsoever to get into competitive trading. For sure, I wanted to do that as it was the line of business I knew so well and had strong contacts in. Everything had gone in my favour, and I felt like Emilio Barzini, "The wolf" of the family, in this case, masterminding my own freedom. Expecting the worst and hoping for the best with my fingers crossed every step of the way is what helped me through this transition in my life.

With two companies up and running, I was ready! I was fast to realize while working for my uncle that I was like a frog in the well, and coming out of his company made me see endless opportunities. The market was deep. Dubai was happening and happening BIG!

I was in Business; I had plans for my future!!

Chapter 8
Being the Sunshine to Make Hay

I had the time, I had the expertise, I had the contacts, I had the networking, I had the inclination, I had the determination, I had the self-belief, and I had what it took … But did I have the money for it?

We seldom forget in the zeal of youthfulness things that are taught to us and are always around us. Money makes money, this was my tagline to my friends every time we had a business discussion, and this is what I missed to understand—how would I get the funds? How do I connect the missing link to run a successful business operation without funds? All we had was a bit of saving due to some past business transactions; we had some meager funds from my gratuity that I had got and a couple of hard-working talents on my side. Now, all I needed was money 😁!!

That was my focus, but what was the plan?

Discussing this with both my talented dudes was pointless, as I would give them a panic attack. I had to think of something, and I needed to think fast, as I did not want to be out of the market too long to be forgotten.

So, I started contacting my contacts who I thought may invest with me, offering them a fair share in the company. These were the business friends who had encouraged me to leave the job and do something, showing me that they believed in me. But one after the other, I faced disappointments; no one came forward to put the money to their mouth's worth. Suddenly, no one seemed to believe in me anymore, and no one wanted to be a part of my company. They wished me good luck with a story about how they had commitments, how they had already invested in some project a couple of months ago, and they didn't have the funds; it reached a point where I suddenly could read through people.

This taught me the crude reality of the world, but I was really happy none of them accepted my request, as without them, I could have never done it alone. Just to let you know, there were mainly four potential investors I spoke to, out of which one later worked for me, two contacted me asking if they could partner with me, and one I again partnered with a different venture. But as of then, all I had was ME!

So, now, I knew what I had in hand and the limitations and the strengths, and it made it easier for me to plan. It goes without saying that my focus turned to the trading company. Being my core business, it was easier for me to manage, plus no obligations on my previous company made it even easier. I put all my attention on the trading business, making sure it was continuing at a constant pace. A wavy graph was a great achievement instead of spiked fluctuation in sales—some weeks good and some weeks fine. How I planned was a target that the trading company should achieve monthly. Sales could not go below the minimum target, and margins were needed to run a healthy business and also to sustain and grow it gradually. I implemented a simple Excel format where I could see the daily sales, purchases, and profits at the end of the day to help me monitor the revenue and ensure that we were trading goods with reasonable margins and customers who gave us prompt payments. On the other side, with my relationship and contacts, it was not hard to get suppliers whom I had worked closely with to help support me with some payment terms. This helped me rotate money more efficiently and to help generate healthy revenue. With sustainability, the regularity went up on the orders; it was not anymore an erratic business. It took me a good four to six months to streamline the business and to make sure things were consistent, and the focus was on customer satisfaction. We would take deliveries in our car; urgent orders were entertained; it was round-the-clock services where we were available to take orders even in the middle of the night, ensuring delivery the next day. This added a lot of credibility with our customers and helped us increase our basket of items to be delivered to them. Getting new clients was not hard, but limitations due to funds made it challenging.

While I was absorbed in my trading business, what I realized was that the cost of the advertising company was just sitting on my head, and the limitations of funds made it harder to manage two companies at the same time. It started to feel like a big burden to take care of its expenses. The only manner was to help the advertising company come to a sustainable level and then to focus on my trading company as my friend, in his limitations, could not manage to sell. My trading company had reached a sustainable level, plus I was not going to move away from it but just pay a little more attention to the sales and growth of the advertising company. My next target was to bring my advertising company to a sustainable level and ensure it was not sucking out the funds that could easily be added into the turnover of the trading company to generate more income and growth. It was time for me to do something about the issue. I knew the advertising company could sustain better as we were mainly selling skills than products. Maybe I saw the potential for growth in the company, thinking it could reach a level where it could also support my trading company.

Keeping the idea in mind that the returns could be better, I started to focus on the advertising company. Going to meetings with my friend and following up with clients, I asked my friend to take me to all his potential customers and helped him do quotations, share ideas, and understand the business. He was good at creativity; I got him a computer where he practiced and managed Photoshop so he could bag more orders and target some really big companies to add to our profile. Right from Markings on Trucks and buses to naming Trophies and selling stencils and signboards, what I realized was that the orders started coming in, and we had to buy raw material, get the design done either on our PC or through a third party, and get the cutting done if the stickers if they were too large again through a third party or it was done manually by my skilled friend if he could manage. It came to a point where I even started to help him in whichever manner I could, doing work that required little skills, such as simply removing air bubbles from pasted stickers or cleaning the surface before pasting the stickers on a signboard. The business was alive, up and running; all I needed to do was follow-ups. We were up against some giants and companies who had automated pieces of machinery and expert software. The only thing that could help sustain us in the industry was the relationship, the attentiveness to the clients, and the support provided by the timely completion of our job sheets. For this, I was taking my friend everywhere for meetings, training him with sales talks, explaining to him the simplicity of communication from a layman's point of view, and guiding him on how he has to manage the clients. Even though the business reached a sustainable level in a couple of months, what I realized was that due to our limitations in equipment and technology, we needed to go on a slow pace and gradually grow the business, as we could not make an effort to invest too much and had to be patient, plan it, and once the business reached a justifiable level, we could reinvest in it.

Three months of concentration on the advertising business led to an effect on the trading business with limited time for trading. All I was doing was ensuring the business was running smoothly. My brother was on the driving seat in the trading company whereas I was just monitoring it. Until I was confident that the advertising business could take care of itself. Once we reached a point, I spoke to my friend and business partner, explaining to him that I could not be focused full-time on the advertising business as we lacked both skilled manpower and technology, due to which the revenue didn't justify the time and efforts that I had been putting in. I told him that he had to manage from there on and I shall always be available for all the important meetings where he felt my presence was required as I had a more promising business just sitting to its least potential. He hesitantly agreed with me. During those three to four months, I ensured the advertising company was not being a burden to the trading company anymore. This was a milestone achieved; now, I could generate and manage to grow the trading with some extra funds due to the lessened burden.

Funds, though, were still a challenge, but my commitment to having the additional expenses of the advertising company taken care of gave us a little leverage to grow the trading business. We looked for hiring a driver, buying a second-hand van for deliveries, and stocking items that we managed to get a good offer on. This was greatly momentous to us, and we started to manage inventory, the little we had…I was still paying attention to both companies, and slowly but surely, we were growing, and it felt great.

I was learning. The market was deep, and the advantage I had was that people who knew me supported me. The bigger advantage was that the market was booming as Dubai was developing; new restaurants, hotels, and QSRs were being added to our portfolio purely due to the service provided. On the other hand, we managed to close a few big companies for the advertising company and got them on for regular business as well. All was well, and we reached a stage where we started to look at options to import our own stocks.

Dubai, the United Arab Emirates, was always a market that was so diverse, with people from all over the world residing here. It was, has, and shall remain a market where one will always need to import. Having nationalities residing here from over 190 nations, one will always have a need for imported products. Even though this market was and has been dominated by Indians, followed by Pakistanis for decades but the average supermarket crowd during those days were Indians closely followed by the British as Pakistanis' had similar food to Indians and so to fulfill the requirement was not much of a challenge but what came to my attention was that the market had a lot of ethnic food requirements for a community that was growing so fast in the region and that was the Filipino community. My vision for Golden Star International was to grow it horizontally in food service and exports, both of which I managed to do, but in retail, our presence was lacking. So, I choose to start importing Filipino food items in the region and sell them in retail. The choice was not easy; the challenges were different. I was not familiar with the products except for some basic items that I had come across, and I kept wondering if I would be able to sell these items in retail. A chance, did I really need it? Knowing my personality, I would love to get into a new challenge plus an opportunity to learn a new range of products. Getting into this was exciting. I had never known of products like banana ketchup, sweet spaghetti sauce, candies made from dried milk powder (Polvoron), preserved balut…things that an average person who lives in Dubai under the influence of western, Arabian, and subcontinental likings and pallets could not know. This got me more excited and enthusiastic. Getting into these new ranges of products required a lot of learning, and this was thrilling. Plus, the competition during those days for the range was far less, but of course, the risk was high, allowing me to make a better margin on my imports and also helping me to open doors to the retail market as retailers saw the demand was increasing but supplies were not easy to find. I wanted to get into retail, and what could have been a better option? I could see it as a gateway to the UAE retail markets.

Next, I knew we had booked our first container of thirty to forty items, all mixed in a container having a little clue what I was getting into. However, I had confidence; my strength was the belief in myself…the go-for-it, take-the-chance attitude…which has actually taken me a lot farther than one can imagine. I knew I could sell… However, selling to retailers was not my strength, and that actually gave me a boost!! Before we knew it, we had a container arriving at our store in less than 50 days. By then, we already had a tie-up with a company to rent shared storage space, as it seemed the most economical storing option at that time.

As soon as the container arrived, we started to sell it to channels we were already strong and present in. Not to our surprise, a lot of products already had a demand in those sectors, but my challenge was the retail stores, and that was where the aim was with these products. This was when I started meeting retailers in the region…asking for references through my connections, and what helped was some of the trading companies that we were already dealing with had their own retail outlets, which allowed us easy entry. It is important to know whom you know in every industry, and I was never shy to use this opportunity and references. This range of products opened a lot of doors for us, and before we knew it, we started to move our products to some of the known and famous retailers in the country. I started building a network and strong relationships with my clients; some of the supermarket managers supported me like family and stood with me, mentoring me on what products I should import and focus on and what quantities and the seasonality of the range. This gave us encouragement and confidence, plus the additional channel that we always struggled to be in. We were present in the RETAIL and, with new promising relationships, were looking forward to growing in the sector!

All this took a lot of effort, persistence, and hard work. It got me totally involved; I was enjoying the energy, the new connectivity, and above all, the learning and the thrill of doing something I had never done in the past. Learning new things has always been my biggest strength and weakness; I tend to kind of lose focus on everything else, and that was exactly what I did. I started to focus on retail; my brother handled the trading business. He is an amazing doer and has always enjoyed being one. The business was growing, and my focus moved totally towards my company with little or no attention to the advertising company that I thought would be doing fine as my friend, my partner, and my acquaintance must have been handling it with responsibility. But after a few months, when we successfully and completely sold out all our stocks, we booked new orders as we were not expecting the sales to roar, and there was a gap until the new shipment arrived. Everything has a reason, and as my mummy taught me, the reason is always for the best! The gap till the new stocks arrived gave me a window, and during this short pause, I managed to find the time to look into the books of the advertising company to see where we stood.

To my bewilderment, I was shocked to know that the company was sucking into its savings like a bloodsucking leech, and the business had hit ground level. This could be due to a lack of my or my friend's intervention, who had recently tied the knot. Upon questioning, he told me the business had been very low, and he had not been able to close a few deals due to challenges; he started to explain a little too much in elaboration that made me a little suspicious to what was happening in the company during my lack of interference. As I had time before my new container arrived, I started to do surprise visits to the office of my advertising company, checking if emails were replied to, if quotations were entertained, and whether regular clients were followed-up…it was easy to understand my friend/partner was enjoying his honeymoon period for over four months and the timing was just in his favour. With my new first shipment from the Philippines arriving, my total diversion from the advertising company was just taken full advantage of. So, I started questioning and visiting the office regularly, sometimes in intervals of a couple of hours, where I would not find my friend at work. Upon questioning, he always had a reason that he was visiting a client or was at a site doing a job…but I could not see any active job-work or any revenue. It was then that I had to take a call, so I called him out for a drink to discuss about what the future plans of the advertising company were.

To my surprise, during our meeting, my friend was a bit arrogant and very defensive. As the evening progressed, he started being more aggressive, asking me justifications, digging up graves with silly reasons, and asking me clarifications from the past, which were totally irreverent to the topic… All this got me into a kind of a dilemma. I was trying to understand what he was getting at until we reached a point where I asked him openly if he would like to continue in the company or not. Even though he was a fair fifty-fifty partner in the profits and we had joint signatories in the bank, let me remind you that he was still not the official owner/shareholder of the company as the investment was

100% from my side, as mentioned earlier when we had started this partnership and understood a limited liability licensing cost was higher; we had jointly opted to keep the company as a sole proprietor where he would hold the managerial visa and rights for the company. This actually turned out to be a blessing in disguise. To my surprise, he actually asked me a couple of days to get back to me on my question, which made it very evident that he has something up his sleeve and was possibly not bold enough to admit it. Supplying advertising materials required a special skill set, and I already knew I was not the person who could do that kind of job. So, the next couple of days, I started to call people whom I knew in the same line of work, seeking advice and offering mergers/partnerships/equities in the company, not that I knew many, but the few I knew did not agree, and not to my surprise my friend got back to me and as predicted opted an out.

I was a little shaken, and with my brother getting annoyed, reminding me what we had gone through to build this company, how I had trusted my friend and giving him the opportunity, and highlighting all that I had done and all that I should not have, made it even worse. He was upset, and it was obvious, so was I, but it was time to stand together rather than waste energy while trying to point fingers and express annoyance. But clearly, he was in a panic mode, as he knew we neither had the skill set for this job nor the right replacement for our partner. Being in the corner and out of desperation, I called my partner to the office, asking him what his future plans were and explaining to him that we could still continue being friends and we did not need to part, but not once did I remember expressing or reminiscing the past as this was not what I wanted; I did not want him to work for the business as an obligation. Nothing worked; he was just so stubborn and determined to leave. I could not understand…why?

So, I asked him to hand over the company belongings such as the mobile phone, keys to the shop, and the company car keys, a second-hand car that we had bought for him to visit sites. To my amazement, to prove his frustration, he just immediately gave it to me and told me, "I may not be a good salesperson like you, but I admire your energy and the skills to sell and also envy it to an extent, sometimes wishing I would have at least some of those skills but ..." and he stopped, gave a very arrogant look as if to say...try to manage the advertising company without my skills. Either he had some respect deep down for me, or he just lacked the confidence to say it to me directly to the face as he knew me. If I took it as a challenge, I may accept it and opt to go for it and prove to him that I can run the company without him. However, his swallowing of words did not make a difference, I was already prepared for his ungratefulness, and it did not matter anymore anyway!

People feel so irreplaceable they forget everyone is unique, but no one is indispensable. He was wrong at guessing; that I could not replace him; I could have looked for people, streamlined the company, adding more value to it. In fact, I had found a person, too, and was already negotiating. However, I changed my mind. I didn't want to. I already had something that I was happy with, and was looking forward to it, my mind and heart were already so focused that I did not want to burden myself with a vengeance and prove myself for some false ego. I already knew it would not be worth the effort; the growth in my trading company was fast, and I was so focused on it plus, to keep the advertising company alive and kicking, I required at least some special skill sets, and it would consume a lot of my time even if I got the right substitute for him, I would just throw away my precious time. I had nothing to prove to him or anyone else, so why focus on continuing the business for the false meaningless sake of it?

However, my professional self didn't allow me to just disappear from the business, so I switched on the company mobile that he handed over, thinking that I should inform any clients if they called, explaining that we had winded up the operations and also make some courtesy calls to a few prestigious customers I knew. I wanted to call and thank them for their support while informing them that we would no longer be providing services. To my surprise, he had deleted all numbers stored on the mobile, which I felt was very unnecessary as he told me he was repatriating back to India for good, so he had no reason to act this way.

In less than an hour, I got a call on the company mobile he was using; the call was from a stationery printing company asking where they needed to deliver the new business cards and invoices that they had printed. This made all the sense, making it evident why he did it. And also, why he wanted to leave—he had planned to start his own business behind my back. I guess he knew me too little. Had he just told me that he would like to buy out the shares of the company and if he had the confidence to take over the company on his own, I would have put in a crazy bargain for him to take over my shares with an easy payback period. We were friends, and I got him from India during his most difficult challenge and bet my hard-earned money on him. The least he could have done was to be honest with me. But, it was not simple for him to do that; this explained the consistent cash business the advertising company was having suddenly disappeared, and for the last three months, we had not had any cash transactions. He had probably already diverted the business or used the cash to set up the new entity behind my back. This also explained a lot of other things; it was his guilt that didn't allow him to look straight into my eyes to discuss the further progress of our existing advertising company.

The above taught me a lot, even though I didn't lose a lot of money as the initial investment was done very conservatively and also due to my initial inclination to get involved in the advertising business to manage and get sales paid off had helped me recover a substantial part of my investment but I lost a lot of time and efforts that I could have used to help my trading business. I considered this as a price for a viable lessons learnt; some operational costs were still to be settled with little funds left in the bank, but that was soon taken care of.

Things were clearer, and even after all this, when I asked my friend to continue to be friends as we might have chosen different paths as per our preferences, but that did not mean we needed to break the friendship that we have had since childhood, he chose not to continue our friendship and never contacted me again. He never mentioned his plans, and I also never told him about the call I got and that I already knew about his new establishment, which he started from the funds that he certainly swiped behind my back. I didn't want to embarrass him over that plus, I had no proof to prove that except for comparing past records.

It was a clear stab in the back; however, it was a good lesson for me to learn and to understand to never deviate and do something that one's skills are not set for. Don't rely on and invest your money in someone based on their capabilities, even if that person was your childhood school buddy. Above all…what this episode taught me was to learn to move on; you have to accept that some chapters need to be closed without a conclusion, and if it didn't make any sense to you, don't be shy to accept it. There is no point in trying to fix something that was meant to stay broken, and this can be a totally new beginning. It helped me take this opportunity to get my total focus back into my trading business to see how to take it to the next level. My undivided attention was now completely on Golden Star International LLC.

It was time for me to be my own sunshine and make hay!!

Chapter 9
Forget It Enough to Get Over It, Remember It Enough to Never Do It Again!

Wish the title of the chapter was a lesson I had remembered, but as I always say: **"Unless you make the horse sweat it out, you can never get it tamed."**

As my focus was 100% on trading and I kept my mindset to it, the company grew leaps and bounds. We were everywhere, and people started to compare us with the biggest names in the market who had been in the region decades before us. It made me proud when people compared Golden Star with bigger players. To achieve a milestone, we got our trading company to be HACCP certified; this was not mandatory, but we chose to be different and were among the first trading companies in the region to obtain it. This is what was bringing us success and helping us grow. Thinking out of the box helped us gain extra mileage, and our risk-taking capabilities added fuel to the fire, especially during the volatile market conditions. We were in most Star properties working with almost all major retailers, exporting, importing, and distributing. We were everywhere with a sales force hired from Europe, Asia, and Africa; we were diverse both in our range and our reach. This was when I asked my younger brother to join the business with me. He was working for a private company and was a qualified US-certified MBA with a major in finance, and he started taking over what I was doing. Things were going in my favour, and as always kept my thinking out of the box, keeping options open to look for any new opportunities to see how we can better this and make this bigger and stronger. Both my brothers were working hard alongside me, and we were taking full advantage of blind trust and reliability. All the departments were giving their total commitment to a new level, and we started introducing new products and getting into various channels of the food industry, also converting some investments into international trade of stocks, forex, and shares. With this constant growth in mind, we were electrified and at the best of our confidence.

Until one day, when I was travelling to Germany for a food show, I got a call while I was at the airport waiting to board my flight that one of my very close allies, who was working for a strong semi-government-owned organization, handling their hospitality sector resigned from his job. I called him immediately and spoke to him over the phone for over an hour, missing my flight; thankfully, I had the next flight in a couple of hours and was lucky to get my ticket transferred to help me be on time to attend the food show.

The reason for me to express the above is to share the excitement I felt. I started to get new ideas on how we could add more value to our company. The person was experienced, knew his game, and was an expert in handling the hospitality sector, running franchises successfully, creating concepts, and growing, handling, and managing the sector seemed natural to him. This was one of the guys whom I had proposed to be a part of my company when I needed funds during the first stage of struggling for money to help grow the company. He was among the few I had asked to invest, and he had been honest or diplomatic perhaps. to tell me due to some prior commitments that needed to be fulfilled, he would not be able to invest, which was respected, and now life gave me another opportunity to work together with him.

The intentions were very simple. I thought of joining him as a partner to start a hospitality business that eventually would buy items from my trading company and then franchise the model in and around the GCC region, create my own brand of food products as per standards set for these concept restaurants and its franchise and supply them securing a long, strong win-win business model. It was a great idea. If this worked, it would be a self-sustained business model with great long-term potential.

After my trip from Germany, which was planned with a short vacation in Europe, all I could dream was of having my own chain of restaurants that one day I would franchise, both nationally and around the GCC nations to start with, then targeting markets like India and parts of Africa. My trading company would source and sell goods to them. This was so exciting and seemed like a foolproof plan. I could not wait to go back to Dubai and meet my future business partner!

When I landed in Dubai, without wasting any time, I asked my friend to meet up to share and understand what he thought of the idea. We met the very next day, where I expressed myself to him. Things got super exciting as it looked like he could relate to me and understand what I was expressing to him. But his intentions were not the same, even though he never stopped me from expressing myself and showed me he shared similar ideas. He had another plan: He wanted to start a Coffee Training Institute in the region, the very first of its kind. I was a little lost, but he explained that there were no institutes training baristas in the region, and with the coffee culture spreading like wildfire in the region, it was an opportunity that we could tap into and become the region's first internationally certified and accredited institute. He had done his spade-work even though this was not what my plan was, but at times, one needs to lose the battle to win the war, so I discussed it with my brothers and took the bait to get closer to my eventual aim. Not that I did not believe in the project, but my focus was something bigger.

We successfully started the first Coffee Training Institute in the region, but my new business partner, even though being a legal entity in the company, chose to stay with a full-time consultancy job to manage a restaurant business with another third party stating he did not want to burden the new company that we started by taking a salary from it. I was against it as I always believed in jumping into the pool to learn to swim. *One can't watch others and learn to swim without getting wet.* He made it sound as if he was protecting the interest of the company I could not accept this but I bought it. I did suggest moving the consultancy under the training institute and taking his revenue through the company itself, which he was reluctant to do. Now when I think of it, perhaps, in a way, he lacked confidence in his own creation. However, it was a new venture, a new partner whom I was always looking up to, so I half-heartedly accepted his decision even though it was something that could never be agreed in my mind.

As time passed, we started to get more clients; reputed hotels, café shops, and brands started to try to associate with us, and we started to get popularity in the region, bagging a few fabled clients in and around the neighbouring countries. The business started to take shape; we built a good reputation and had a dynamic team that took the initiative to do so. But to pursue the restaurant business was still firm in my head, and I was slowly sculpturing towards my target. By now, my new business partner also started to gel well; he started to have more confidence in our partnership, but all this was short-lived as one of our star sales heads had to leave due to her personal commitments, and she was handling a lot of our major/prestigious clients. This was when I strongly advised my partner to take the leap and jump into the business, as the time was ripe and the opportunities were many. To my surprise, he did not accept my proposal and instead hired another person to take full responsibility for the business and continued to consult a third-party restaurant business. It was very weird for me to accept this; however, his first judgment with the set-up went well, so I had no ground to doubt or question him on his call. As long as he managed the business well and we were seeing results, I guessed he knew better what he was doing, so I allowed the changes to happen without my interference.

It didn't take long to see that the business was not the same anymore and that the new person was trying but was not able to take care of it in the same manner. This made me panicky, and I asked my partner to roll up his sleeves and get his hands into the business. And that was what he did; he moved from his consultancy job into the Coffee Training Institute. I still remember his statement, "My mom always advised me to park my ass where my money was!" Even though he had a very minuscule investment in the business, I didn't know why suddenly he just agreed to my proposal when I had been suggesting the same many times earlier. Well, whatever it was, I was happy that he did until I came to know a month later that the restaurant he consulted already had plans to sell off, and he knew his consultancy would not be required or he had already been told to discontinue his services. But at that moment, for me, him coming on board was a great achievement. His coming on board did not make much change to the Coffee Training Institute as I had anticipated. He kept pushing the new guy, guiding him, and mentoring him but never took the reins in his own hands. The whole concept in the region was new, and yes, initially, it did click due to enthusiasm, but it quickly died off.

This taught me that: It is not always that the early bird who gets the worm… Too early, and the bird might just get tired waiting for the worms to come out. I had a full-fledged trading business to run, and I could not find the time to contribute to this business except to just promote it with word of mouth, and connect the guy for coffee training to potential customers. The business showed some momentum but nothing substantial.

However, it did not take much time before my partner started to show interest in my proposal of having a restaurant; things were falling too quickly into place. It could be because he, too, felt we needed to initiate new ideas as things were not working out with the training institute, but I was too naïve to see that. He kept a term that he wanted to have a fixed withdrawal from the company to support his lifestyle/livelihood/living… I was very new to the whole business and overexcited with my plan to grow, and, in many ways, ignorant as this was not my line of expertise. I totally trusted the capabilities of my new partner and believed he was an honest person. But life taught me in a very crude manner that **"Being Honest"** and **"Being Fair"** are <u>**two different things**</u>, and even though my partner seemed totally honest, it did not make him fair with his proposal but being inexperienced, I was trusting his capacity, my faith in his capabilities and also taking him as a mentor in many ways. I had total faith that he would be fair. I spoke to my brothers and made them agree with me. We accepted all his proposals to set the dream of our first Hospitality Outlet that I wanted to initiate and grow. The excitement was tremendous! My partner did warn me, though, that it shall not be easy and we would require a lot of funds, at which I suggested – "Let's move slowly and progressively take one step at a time; we can work on things together and grow this to a new level," reminding him of my idea that was proposed at the start.

We started to look for places where we could start something small. Things were slow, tiring, and exhausting; it was not easy, as people didn't believe in us. The coffee institute was not doing all that great anymore, and it was clear that that was the main reason that had initiated my partner to move faster into the new venture. I could see his genuine efforts that made me feel happy, thinking that it all happens for a good reason, and finally, he was into it!

Then, we found a place, a place that was perhaps a mammoth with an Eighty-Seated capacity, but the place was at that time the most happening and growing place in town. We got all excited, and he was a pro at it. Not cutting corners, he put all his efforts into it. It was a great learning experience to see him work with his passion, the thoughts and the ideas behind the creation, and the dedication, I was enjoying the build-up, and I was so passionate that this was finally happening. The work started on everything—logos, the menu, the recipes. Even though he kept me in the know, he preferred to have his own space to work, and I never got into his territory unless he would ask for a suggestion, possibly to make me feel important at times. Anyway, I always respect a professional at his work, and I never step on an area that I already know is managed well.

However, always remember: Humans have two kinds of mentalities: a dog mentality, where a person thinks if he is treated right, loved, and respected, the people who are kind to him are divine souls; and then there are those who have a cat mentality where they think if they are treated right, loved, and cared for, they must be a divine soul. My trust, high regard and respect towards my partner's experience and skills were taken by my partner, similar to the cat mentality.

Chapter 10
Buy Skills, Don't Get Bought by It

An important lesson in business: While hiring skills don't lose your sense of proposition, don't allow someone else's skills to influence you to the extent that you overprice them. **Every skill has a price** depending on various factors like the role it plays, the efforts and above all, the returns one gets from hiring it.

Remember, no matter how talented the person's skills or abilities are, until there is a buyer for it, it has no worth. So, if you are the buyer, remember to price it right. One can easily get carried away. Simultaneously, the talented/skilled person can also never get their worth without the right buyer. There has to be a balance, without which it would not be a fair proposition. With all the excitement and the feeling that I had the best skill in the industry as my partner, I never wanted to let go. Impressed by his past achievements, I gave him a lot more credentials than even he had expected.

Anyway, the day finally arrived, and we opened our first restaurant in town—it was a beauty. I was a bit involved with things like the colour of the logo; the name, of course, was suggested and accepted, and things looked like a dream had come true. After we opened, the place looked so posh, so elegant, that it took a few days for people to actually walk into the place. I remember calling the place and asking how many customers did we have today? This I used to do every day until the restaurant gradually started picking and people relished our food. It was truly value for money. The whole idea was to get loyalty from the customers. And things started to change so fast that before we knew it, we had a waiting list during lunch hours. My dream came true, and my business partner was floating on cloud nine!

Things were moving well. Even though we were not breaking even with the training institute, we were seeing progress with the restaurant…but like all businesses, you have to be in it until you can make an effort to be on it. My partner's vision was not to have just one restaurant but to have a chain of restaurants. However, to start with it, we needed the first one to be a success in my opinion. I had a similar view to him, but after we invested much more than budgeted for in the first restaurant, the return on investment would take much longer than anticipated. Plus, we were not gaining any profit from the training institute. It was a dead investment that was lying totally stagnant. We even tried using the sales head of the training institute as the restaurant manager, allowing him to justify his salary. We thought he would manage well as he had a rich background as a restaurant manager and was an ex-hotelier. All of a sudden, the only focus seemed to be on the new restaurant venture. However, our plan to use the sales-head for the dual role did not work. He could not manage both portfolios, and he seemed to have lost the inclination, so finally, under pressure to perform, he opted to move on, and we gladly allowed that.

The restaurant business was doing good, and it was time to press the gas, but what surprised me was that my partner was just going with the flow when it was time to really work harder and get things to new heights and challenging each day. I felt he was in his easy chair, drawing his fixed salary (living allowance that we had mutually agreed upon), and the efforts were not as a business owner but just as a good employee.

Some people have a very small appetite, and a bit of success makes them feel great and satisfied. This reminds me of my younger brother's favourite quote of

all time from Steve Jobs: "Stay Hungry, Stay Foolish!" This is the key to the growth of any business. If your business is doing great, it's time for you to accelerate, not relax.

Shortly after, my business partner got a good job offer to manage one of the well-known and fast-growing companies in the region handling industrial bakeries and multiple other businesses. He rejected the offer even though it paid him much more than the living allowance that he was drawing. He told this to me and made it look like he did me a big favour. I kept silent, but I was astonished—why? Could he not see the opportunity I had given him? He got much more than a fair share, an equal partnership, a fifty percent stake of my hundred percent investment. Buying a concept would have cost me a fraction in compression to the value of shares I had given him. But even though he rejected the offer, I had no reason to doubt that it clearly changed his focus on our present business.

FOCUS: Follow **O**ne **C**ourse **U**ntil **S**uccessful, but my partner was not focused, and he got easily diverted. In delusion that he lost a growth opportunity by rejecting the proposal, he became totally blind to what he already had with him; he had an opportunity of a lifetime, an opportunity not many are privileged to get. He could make the best of it with his set of skills to manage and grow, which would not be very challenging, especially for a man of his experience and knowledge. This got me under tremendous pressure from my partner. He started to build up that pressure, always talking about his opportunity loss, which by the way, he would have never gotten in the first place without the success of this restaurant. **"The one that tastes success too quick cannot relish its true taste!"**

A lot of money, way over our budget, had already been invested in this eighty-seater mammoth flagship store and going with the flow and the excitement of our first restaurant, I admit we went overboard. But the business was good, yet we needed more time to recover our investment. Until then, we had to manage to run it in the same way. However, with the pressure from my partner to protect our investment along with the hope of returns and to keep my partner happy, I agreed to an expansion even though the additional investment would stress us out. I discussed this with my brother with a positive and fighting spirit to go ahead.

In the meantime, we also tried to franchise the existing restaurant and look for new investors and potential partners for the new concepts, but everything looked like a carrot hanging right in front of our eyes, yet too far from our reach. The pressure was tremendous! My business partner, although a genius at building concepts, lacked the skill to promote and sell them. He was an amazing chef, a creator, master in his line of work, and yet when it came to selling his own creation, he lacked the knack for it. His issue was not that he was not confident; his issue was that he was overconfident and expected people to understand his concept straight away, stating if they didn't, they were not the right clients for it. I saw him as the 21st-century Vincent Van Gogh. Mr. Gogh's paintings only got famous 20 years after he died, and he was only able to sell one painting during his whole life. My partner almost never introduced me to potential buyers or leads, perhaps feeling that he was the best person to sell his own creation. He was underestimating me, or he was overestimating my skill. If I broke the deal, he would not get the credit for it. I really don't know what he was thinking. We were business partners and not competitors.

Based on the above facts and also the emphasis of my partner, who kept reminding me how he was losing time, missing great opportunities, and might even consider working for other companies if we didn't start investing into opening more restaurants and concepts soon. Not to mention the recent success of our restaurant that gave him an additional boost of confidence, adding another feather to his cap. He also convinced me that the restaurant business was all about the number of outlets; neither he nor we would grow with just one restaurant. **"It is always easier to conquer the injured!"** and I was lost. It seemed at that moment that the only appropriate way to secure my investment was to pump in more investment. Left with little choice, I opted to take my chances, accepting his proposal of investing more into the restaurant business.

Chapter 11
It Is Always for the Best!

The growth opportunity for my trading business still seemed tremendous while I was struggling with my training and restaurant businesses. Trading was always my blue-eyed baby and also the only cash cow for my survival; I could not ignore it. With my new commitments now, I could no longer inject funds into Golden Star International; rather, the new business commitment started to drain money from it. Time had once again put me in a spot where I started to look for a potential investor to grow the trading business. I started discussing this with very close friends and family.

The opportunity was seen by one of my mother's cousins, another uncle of mine, who had been working for a very strong company in the region since forever and had the funds to invest, but he wanted his young and energetic son to be a part of it and learn the trade. He had tried with a few people, but no one wanted to teach their business line as they perhaps saw future competition with them.

But in my case, my uncle was very close and a person I could trust. My mother, a single child, considers him as her sibling even though they are just cousins. Plus, the way the challenges were growing for Golden Star was always at the back of my head. So, taking the opportunity, I opted to allow my uncle to invest, not in my main trading company but in a branch that we jointly opened in the Emirate of Abu Dhabi, which was always our dream. What an irony—on the one hand, I invested with my partner in the restaurant business and on the other side, I involved my uncle to invest in my trading business to open a new branch.

Things started to move smoothly; we made a branch office in Abu Dhabi, and trading being our strength and expertise, it didn't take much time to excel. Things moved hard and fast, and our operation started in no time. On the other side, we built concepts for the new restaurants and decided to start in one of the known yet not among the most visited malls in Dubai. The excitement was ecstatic, with the hope that things would fall in place with this new approach. All this cost us a lot of money and time, and the day finally came for us to start our restaurant. With all positivity and new aspirations, we were full of energy and radiance.

Things moved well, and in the first few months, the reviews of our restaurants were amazing. Everyone who visited our restaurant complimented its meals, the service, and the presentation. We were going to revolutionize the QSR (Quick Service Restaurant) business in the region. The feedback was great, and even my frequency to the place increased as I was taking all business allies to our outlets. People loved it, and the shine in my eyes and the throbbing of my heartbeat, hearing all the kind compliments everyone gave, truly made me proud. The sense of achievement was overwhelming. Things went well for the first year in terms of reviews, feedback, quality, loyal clients, and repeated customers. Everything seemed par excellence; however, we still faced an issue with the footfall in the mall. As I said, the mall was very well-known yet not a popular one for visitors. The footfall to the mall was few, and even though we had a gem of restaurants, sales were a challenge.

Sustaining with low business was getting more and more challenging. Things started drifting apart as new restaurant businesses were not generating enough revenue, and we kept losing money. We had commitments on rentals, salaries, renewals of visas and licenses, and operation costs. All this could not be recovered with the business these restaurants generated. Our very first flagship, the eighty-seated restaurant, which was doing good, also started to lose business as little to no attention was given to it by my partner. His mind got diverted to the new concepts, and it seemed that after receiving great compliments, success hit his head. It felt as if he went into a kind of an "I am…" mode, and no one else can!

I believe there is a very thin line between confidence and overconfidence. "Confidence is 'I can do it', overconfidence is '<u>Only</u> I can do it!'" Overestimating oneself and underestimating the rest is always a dangerous state of being.

The whole idea was never about testing my partner's deliverance or his skills; it was about the concept, a concept that should make money at the end of the day to attract people, franchise it, and grow it. It made absolutely no sense to have great amazing restaurants for people to come and praise them. Instead of feeling the financial pinch and making a desperate attempt to fix it, he chose to keep hiring restaurant managers, one after the other. He kept hiring and firing; he kept making excuses and reasoning as to why things were not working instead of trying ways and means to make it work. Every time we had meetings, they used to be long, tiresome, endless discussions, and the next day, I would come to know that he was travelling on a short vacation due to public holidays. That showed a lack of attention and concern. He could not feel the financial strain we were going through or rather opted to conclude that it was just not his problem when in ground reality, it was. He was our partner, and it was most definitely a mutual setback—If we won't grow, so won't he, as business partners are always related as one.

It seemed like my brothers and I were the only people concerned about the restaurant business, rightly so, it was our investment, and we were feeling the pain. It reached a point where I was going and sitting on weekends in front of my restaurant, trying to analyze where things were going wrong. The additional restaurants allowed my partner to show the world that he was a great success on the outside, but the crude reality was that none of the restaurants were generating revenue. Every time I spoke to him to get more involved, he used to show this tremendous superiority as if to show, 'Don't step into my territory; if you know better, do it yourself'. To discuss issues with him became a huge challenge for me. All of a sudden, my partner had become – Onaga, the Dragon King from Mortal Kombat, and it seemed like I was battling with all my skills to show him the actual reality and he was like a major antagonist.

Later on, he started to avoid me; we hardly met, and he was always busy with discussions. Every time I fixed an appointment, he had prior commitments. I could not see what was more important than our business. I had a full-time commitment with my trading company, yet I would make time for him; I let no opportunities go without trying, my business was sinking, and I needed to save it. During our good past, we used to meet twice a week, now when the situation was desperate, we started to meet only once in three months, that too only for official company meetings to discuss the restaurants. I could see my partner take the first opportunity he would get to avoid the meeting as he did not like being questioned. Life had brought me once again to the same spot when I felt the arrogance and that sense of one feeling indispensable, the same manner my partner in the advertising company felt, but this time, I had a lot more at stake!

All of a sudden, to me, his knowledge, experiences, and preaching all seemed to be nothing more than loose talk, and he looked helpless and weak as he could not manage the challenge he was facing. Running away from it and avoiding me was not the solution. I don't even know if he could see what I was going through or the opportunity he had, which still could be fixed and help us grow mutually. I always say, **"Unless you see it as an opportunity, it is just going to sit there and rot!"** We are always told opportunities are created, but we often forget to look around for them. Star Bucks sells coffee waste as fertilizers, which is a brilliant idea, and here we had a concept that people loved, and all we needed to do was to work the right formula and create an opportunity instead of an excuse.

Things were not getting any better, and I was panicking, so privately, I started to look for someone who could run the business for us as a last option. I started to meet a lot of people, but I could not find anyone that met the needs, requirements and expertise as my present partner. It is not impossible, but always hard to replace a person who has grown organically with the business and knows the business right from the root level. Plus, I didn't want to jump into the fire from the frying pan; I could not afford to make any more mistakes and needed to take every step with caution.

I remember during one of the meetings with a consultant, one of many I met. He gave me a piece of advice, stating, "It's your money; the way you will work for it, no one else will..." Seeing my timid attitude towards the restaurant business, he continued saying, "...What if your partner died tomorrow?"

This was a wake-up call; it shook me from the inside. Things were bad. It came to a point where my brothers and I got desperate. I proposed in a meeting to shut down an outlet that was draining us the most. To my surprise, my partner didn't even blink an eye when this was suggested; he just agreed! What was even a greater shock to me was when he calmly replied, "It's your call..." This got me in a mode where I had to put my foot down, and the first thing that was done was to stop my partner's fixed income that he was still drawing from our trading company. We were losing money by buckets, and someone had to be held accountable for it. When he asked me about it, I replied to him in the same calm manner as he did, "Make money to take money!"

It was after years that I saw him changing. He started to listen to our options and proposals but somehow never actually implemented them. We were bleeding and bleeding to near death, and this required an emergency fix. The pressure was tremendous, and we wanted to stand and fight together as a team. But it didn't take me time to find out the truth behind his silence. As I say, **"The strong have an attitude, the weak have an ego!"** It was the silence of his ego. And <u>a silent ego is the most profound of all</u>. He had started to look for other opportunities and was planning an exit from the situation, like a rat fleeing a sinking ship!

All this diverted my focus and attention from my trading business. Now that is what I would call a real opportunity loss. We were struggling; we were burning out the rope of hope from both ends.

The good news was during that time, the new venture, in which my uncle and his son had partnered with us in Abu Dhabi, was going pretty well. Yes, his son was smart but lacked a sense of maturity; it could be because of the absence of experience or just the zest of youthfulness, but as long as he was managing the business, it did not bother me. So, I decided to go talk to my uncle, asking him for support and help us fund the trading business as this was the most successful business we owned and yet had a lot of potentials. This time the investment was not for the Abu Dhabi branch but for the mother-company itself, which still had great prospects; despite all the challenges, it was still generating profits. I offered him a fixed percentage of returns for the funding, which I could see he was not pleased with. So, I asked for his proposal and was expecting an offer from him. I kept thinking perhaps he would ask for a larger stake in the Abu Dhabi Company. Or maybe a stake in the mother-company… In all reality, I was expecting some support, considering he was a part of the company and he would want to help us for mutual success. But I judged wrong. **"A hyena does not bring food to the weak!"** The way I see it, they lost a great opportunity. Thinking like a businessman, I would have never lost this chance, perhaps demanding to inject funds for a larger stake in the branch or even grabbing the opportunity to be a partner in the mother-company itself. After all, they had experienced my growth, as they were part of the family. But, **"When the intentions are not virtuous, the mind is destructive, and a destructive mind is never a progressive one!"**

One has to be blessed to have such people in life; not supporting me helped me be stronger. Thanking my lucky stars, they could never see the opportunity time provided to them. My uncle and his son opted to part from our Abu Dhabi partnership upon renewal of its business license, and as one can easily predict, the son started a competitive company, even copying the initials of our company name.

Nothing surprises me in life anymore; this episode, too, was taken by my brothers and me very sportingly. When my mother heard this, she looked into my eyes and asked me if I was okay. <u>"Yes, Ma'am. Fitter and Stronger than ever before!"</u> was what I replied with a smile looking straight into her eyes - She felt it too!

In reality, I really was. They missed the opportunity, and that was all I could see. They were not able to exploit my circumstances which was a blessing. Leaving me to fight my own battle was the best thing the universe gifted me, making me stronger and more vigilant and giving me and my brothers confidence and power to face any and every situation. As Zig Ziglar said, "It is not how far you fall, but how high you bounce that counts," and from this experience, I add – **<u>"To bounce back high, one needs to fall hard!"</u>**

I made desperate attempts to see the light at the end of the tunnel for my restaurants, but it was already too late. It came to a point where I didn't know if I had to struggle to save a sinking ship or save myself to perhaps build a new one again someday. All the great business jargon from my restaurant partner was meaningless, and he safely fizzled out of all financial commitments. To my surprise, when I started to manage the business and tried a few new things in my restaurants, it added a little spark to the business even though I am not an expert in the field. It only proved to me that if focused, we could have saved the businesses and perhaps grown it too. Plus, 'No one will take care of your investment as you will'. The words of the consultant still ring in my ears and shall always remain in my heart and mind. During my attempts to run the restaurants, I realized we had so many options to make the restaurants a success. Right from home deliveries, tie-ups with dark kitchens, and evening ladies' parties with a rented kids' play area, our place was spacious with a lot of free parking space. The possibilities seemed endless, but again, the time required to repair, recover and run was not worth the effort; hence, we opted to close all our restaurant businesses and go back to what we were best at.

When it comes to business, one has to be open-minded. At times we get the most brilliant ideas from amateurs. Don't ever let your ego take over you. Whatever you try to prove under the influence of your ego is pointless, temporary and takes you nowhere. Even without my partner, I managed to run the restaurant business for over a year before we decided to wind up, another example proving the possibilities it held.

Being left with the trading company, still holding my biggest asset with me, it was time again to put all attention on Golden Star International. More than ever before, it now needed time, investment, focus, and commitment.

It's not that during challenging times nothing goes right; it was during these struggling times that I had an opportunity to start working closely with someone who had come to me stressed with a challenge. One of her shipments was rejected in Jordan by the Food and Drug authorities due to sudden changes in regulations; she came to me with a kind of belief in me, asking for help. I genuinely wanted to help her out; I could and did opt to do so. Starting to interact and work with someone that seemed honest, fair and, above all, a practical business thinker. She was none other than the Green Tea enthusiast, who, after all these years, still is: **Ms. Nadiya Albishchenko!**

Chapter 12
Investing in Oneself

Being a small-town girl from Mykolaiv and the only child to my parents, I have grown up to stand up for myself. From the early stages of my life, it came to my understanding that **the most important person I should believe in is myself,** for if I don't, who will? Through the challenges of time, the most important factor that has helped enhance and develop me was the fact that I trusted in myself and kept investing in myself, and that has led me to being what I am today.

From a very early age, I was fascinated with the skills of my grandma, who was into network marketing, selling cosmetics through her contacts, trading with friends and relatives, being very popular communally, and having a chain of followers. I believe she was someone who helped me with my desire to have my own business set-up one day.

If I try to reminisce, I was interested in business from a very young age. My first business was to collect bubble gum cards with car images from a popular chewing gum brand, 'Turbo'; every kid was doing that, but I enjoyed eating the chewing gum and was not keen on collecting cards. These cards had a picture of a car and some details about it.

I remember selling the cards to my friends, thereby creating my own childhood trading network. The best times were when I got lucky getting some rare Turbo collections, those that were in demand. I would exchange them for two chewing gums or even sell them at an extra cost so I could buy more Turbos. I had created a kind of chain trade deal. It was very interesting and exciting; I was able to convince a lot of kids to buy from my collection as they could choose the cars they wanted instead of depending on their luck and getting cars that were either not of their choice or were repeats. I was greatly fascinated and very serious about my business. What seems a child-like play was probably something that gave me an early inspiration to do my own business. Hence, the memory of it is so clear in my head, even today.

While growing up, I always looked for alternative sources of income. My grandma showed me simple ways of how I could make my own pocket money. I used to collect empty bottles from the beach, wash and sell them for recycling, to get petty change, and this small change collected every day would make a decent sum of money, especially for a kid my age. I felt a bit shy about collecting bottles in front of the public, so the main target was to go and search for them during dusk when there was still enough light to see, yet less crowd on the beach. If I got lucky, I would find some other interesting things too. I remember once I found a huge floating mattress that someone had forgotten on the beach, and I played with it for months. There was a public washing station in front of the beach condos, where some like-minded kids and I used to wash our daily collections. It was hard-earned pocket money, and the best part about it was I could spend it the way I wanted to; it was my stash, after all. This gave me a sense of freedom and the inclination encouraging me to keep doing it.

Living in the USSR had its moments. I remember being a proud Octobrist as a child, and then suddenly, everything collapsed in a few months. An independent Ukraine was formed. This was a big change. August 24, 1991, was an experience one could never forget, even for a child. The changes were so rapid, and the country had to go through the most challenging economic phase. Change in government, currency, privatization process, segregation of assets from Russia, new strategies and policies, and many such challenges lay before young, Independent Ukraine. My family was no exception and suffered financially, as the struggle was so immense. I still remember my family could not afford to buy meat, and my mother kept inventing recipes to substitute meat in our meals.

Despite all changes that happened, my entrepreneurial interest continued to mushroom even more now than ever, mainly because I had to help myself manage my own pocket money. I started to learn the works of the best Russian writers and poets at school and created a team with my clones, who had similar thinking and desires. Together, we created a group consisting of young performers who could sing and dance and had skills such as art and crafts, drawing, etc. We used to organize weekend performance shows and exhibitions in the neighborhood yard. My part was to read my poems with bold expressions. I developed well and used to perform commendably during the shows. As entertainment was limited and parents liked to encourage their kids, almost all of the neighborhood used to come to our event. We were even drawing tickets to sell it to them. After the end of each event, we would count the earnings and used to buy treats from a famous bakery in the locality, which offered privileged pricing for us performers. These moments are among the sweetest memories of my childhood days.

Organizing the event and practicing my part in the show helped me better my skills, thus, enhancing my performance at school. This aided an increase in my grades, making me among the toppers in the class. Also, organizing the events helped me develop leadership and team-building skills at a very young age, and I continued to take the responsibility of being a good, studious student and a class leader for almost all of my primary schooling years.

During early academics, I had the option to learn a foreign language. I chose to study English. As kids, we had a slang in Russian – 'London is the capital of England'. It was a phrase that caught my attention, though I am not sure of its origin or the actual meaning of it, even now. But, it influenced me in a very profound manner. It made me start to dream about visiting London one day. I wanted to visit London; in fact, I wanted to see the world. I got so obsessed with the desire and believed that the English language would be the key to my aspiration. So, I set my mind to learn the language. I started to focus on the language with total dedication…reading, writing, practicing new words, talking to myself and faking accents from Hollywood movies in front of the mirror. Not many were as encouraged or fascinated with the language as I was. It came to a point where it had become an obsession. I was reading books all day until late at night, trying to learn new phrases, and practicing pronunciations and terminologies. I made myself believe that this was the only way I could achieve my dream of seeing the world, and I was very serious about it!

After completing ninth grade, I got my admission to the economical lyceum, where studies were much more challenging compared to that in a normal government curriculum. We had additional subjects like accounting, bookkeeping, and economics besides the regular school syllabus. In the last year of academics, we had to submit an individual project by making a presentation on one of the various subjects provided. This was a very important project as it affected the annual grades of the students. I, chose – 'Establishing New Business' – as a topic for the project.

My presentation was based on owning a high-end Italian shoe shop for men and women. I was completely immersed into the project, covering every aspect of it…marketing strategies, detailed expenditures, such as cost of goods, operational expenses, storage and shop rentals, and detailed profit and loss calculations. All this was backed with complete facts, right from buying the material to finally selling it to the end consumer. The project had a full forecast on sales, stocks, budgeting, and even future enhancement of the business.

This project is so important for me to talk about because, at that time, it took me forever to complete it. I spent endless hours in the library, reading Business books and discussing the project with my working mother, who, although not an entrepreneur, had her exposure and experience in the work environment. She, with her limitations, helped me with some basic factors. I started reading business magazines from her workplace to get new, better ideas on modern methods of business, supplementing the traditional business ideas from books in the library. This project helped me understand more in detail about how a modern establishment works. The efforts were genuine, and so were its rewards. My professor, also a renowned businessman in the area, loved my presentation to such an extent that he offered me a chance to work for his company as a part-time employee, thus, giving me my very first job.

This was amazing as I was looking for an opportunity to work and help support myself financially so that I could enroll myself at the university. As a student, it was one of my biggest achievements. Now, I not only got the opportunity to work and earn, but also I could look forward to my future education. It was a proud moment! Knowing the challenges my parents were facing, I knew they could not support my further education. I felt so blessed!

My first work experience taught me a lot of patience and how to be observant. On my first working day, I was asked just to sit and observe people and what they do in the office…how they communicate. In short, I was just asked to get a feel of being a part of the team. I felt very awkward coming into an environment where I had to be sober and just patient. It felt like I knew nothing; everyone was talking using a very different vocabulary. A lot of terms and expressions that I had never heard were being used, and I could not make sense of them. It took me a little time to get used to the communication, but knowing myself, learning new things and taking up challenges is what I was born for.

I started to socialize and blend with my colleagues during lunchtime and coffee breaks, checking their job profiles and what they were doing. I started learning new things from them, showing interest in every department to understand the structure of the company and its functions. Within a year, I was completely involved in the company operations, dealing with creditors, management, making trade deals, and managing accounts. Soon I became an integral part of the group. I had a lot of energy and passion; I was hungry to learn and wanted to find new ways of improvising things. I did not want to just play the role of a fancy piece of furniture in the office and keep following the traditional attitude of doing a monotonous job. So, I started to innovate, change, and share my ideas with the management and the team. A lot of them were implemented into the company's system, making me feel very confident about myself.

My very first job, my self-development, made me feel I was at the top of the world. I expected to have some extra monetary benefits. Hence, I approached the management to request an increment that I so rightly deserved. The management did not accept my request. I felt exploited, as I knew I was putting real hard work and genuine efforts into the company. It was time for me to move on. I already had confidence in myself and knew I could get better opportunities. Plus, my focus still remained fixed on international exposure.

It wasn't long before I got an offer for the position of food cost controller in a recreational facility during the summer. My new role meant new learning, plus a place to work on the lakeside, with a breathtaking view from my balcony. I have always been a fast learner, and my curiosity and eagerness are the blessings that get the credit for it.

If you feel you are exploited and you are sure about yourself, you have to take your chances. It is important for you to earn your value. It is also important to evaluate and price yourself right. This will always help you to grow in the right manner. Pricing yourself right would not only help you to boost your self-confidence but shall also allow you to enhance. My desire to have a higher income was always an important part of my inspiration. This has always helped me to keep developing myself and move up the ladder of success.

Chapter 13
Attempt to Be a Jack of all Trades

I was young, enthusiastic, inquisitive, curious, and eager to learn, and the only major commitment I had was the university admission fee. For that, I had already planned savings in case of a rainy day.

I started to take explorative opportunities to enhance the experiences that would help mould me and shape me for a better tomorrow. With different work experiences, I gained different expertise. Working with the walnut factory allowed me to understand the whole process of export operations, warehouse management and how to calculate the hourly wages of the workers, as well as job control processes. Cosmetic trading taught me how to look at and approach clients through telesales, thereby improving my negotiation skills. As I was growing up, the one experience that was the most valuable was working for the bank.

Working as a deputy of chief accountant in a bank at a very young age is a job that people would die for in many countries, as also in Ukraine. It was a dream job that was prestigious, respected and a profile that one would be proud of. At the start, I was astonished at my achievement; it was unbelievable and something I thought I would never leave. Even though it was a great experience, with time, I was quick to realize it was a very monotonous job, and one had to dedicate so much time and energy to it that by the end of the day, it drains you out. One was left with no life beyond work… Sleepless nights especially before national bank audits, making reports, endless papers on papers, assembling all files, massive accounting books, reconciliations, and salaries.

Everything was manual in those days in Ukraine, consuming a lot of time, with long working hours and time-bound pressures. One could hardly manage time even to study, let alone personal development or gatherings with friends or relatives. All work and no play! Thus the feeling that life was coming to an end started to grow within me. But I was not going to quit so easily. I used the opportunity to learn and learn more, and the experience helped me get connected with many business owners, helping me grow my network and connectivity in the right manner.

One of the governors in our city had set up a company for his wife and was our client at the bank. I was his account manager; he had a lot of transactions and very often used to pay a visit to the bank to complete the paperwork. We would usually talk and discuss different subjects, and one day casually, I shared my vision of getting international exposure. He was well-connected, and he always used to praise and appreciate my work, determination, and the prompt services that were provided by me when he visited the bank. He recommended me to a large establishment having sparkling beverages that were manufactured in Odessa and were being exported to many parts of the globe.

Odessa was less than two hours' drive from where I lived, and through his recommendation, I managed to get a new job as an export administrator in the company with a much better pay cheque. This happened mainly due to my English language skills. I jumped at the opportunity provided, as it was my first step towards my dream, a desire that I had, right from my childhood, my desire to travel. I was super excited and started dealing with clients; my English skills were not all that great, as I needed to practice. Over a period, it started improving as day after day; I was communicating with our overseas customers, interacting, discussing, negotiating, and finally, my first opportunity was an earned trip to Moscow as an exhibitor representing my company.

With the tickets in my hands and a big smile on my face, the excitement was beyond expression. My very first experience of getting into an aeroplane, getting a window seat, was the icing on the cake. This was exactly the way I had always imagined it would be. It was a very small and noisy plane, but I was not bothered about it. I did not even know that I was flying in the business class and that, along with me, was also the national basketball team who were flying to Russia. Well, I was never a basketball enthusiast, so I thought it would have been better if I could have had the opportunity to meet other people who were linked to international trade, but that's beside the point. My excitement level was so high that as the flight took off, it felt as if the butterflies in my stomach would pop out of my mouth!

It was my first ever travel abroad, and when the meals were served, I just could not believe it! I felt really happy, a feeling of accomplishment, something that I always wanted and had finally achieved; a dream comes true. In practical terms, this was not an achievement but the start of my international exposure, getting me closer to my idea and my ambition to see the world. This trip inspired me and helped me believe in myself more than ever before, helping me lift my ambition to propel myself further in my quest to discover the World.

Bigger opportunities were waiting for me as my search for the better had never stopped. Improvements in the Internet and online searches encouraged me to submit my application and seek jobs abroad. I continued checking different options, conducting numerous online interviews, and exchanging emails, until one day, I got an offer to represent a computer hardware and accessories company as an indoor sales representative in Egypt. I accepted the offer without even discussing it with my parents. I called them to say my goodbyes, and within no time, I again had a window seat on a plane, looking out from my window sill at the snowy hills and gray skies of Ukraine with a shine in my eyes and a wide smile on my face. I was flying out of Ukraine to experience my very first international job.

The Land of the Pharaohs was right in front of my eyes. The new culture, new traditions, and new religion were a cultural shock. But I was still curious and even more eager to learn. I started to slowly learn a few Arabic words to understand the people around me. In just a few months, I was able to communicate simple sentences that would help me with day-to-day communication. I also gained limited reading and writing skills in the language.

The work culture was very new to me; the markets were working on credit terms. How can one supply products without receiving the payment first? I had never experienced such a form of trading in Ukraine. Being a cash-driven market, the customers in Ukraine would never see the face of their goods before the supplier received his full payment. These new ways of working, even though not practically acceptable for a business to me personally, taught me a different culture of business. Cheque payments after presenting Invoice copies and statements at the end of the month didn't seem to make business sense, it was a bit complicated compared to a simple bank transfer before supplies in Ukraine, but soon I grew to understand the policies and procedures and got interested the ways of business in the region.

Over a period of time, I also noticed that the male population in the country was more than the female population, or at least it felt that way. Coming from a country where it was vice versa, it triggered an idea in me. I thought, why could I not start an online matchmaking venue linking genders of both countries and start my own online marriage agency? Seeing an opportunity, I started to investigate the possibilities of establishing the same. I convinced my management to invest in website development and proposed a partnership. My part was to register ladies from Ukraine, and the management's part was to market the site in Egypt. It did not surprise me that they loved the concept and approved the idea; we were in business.

The client needed to pay a registration fee and a recurring monthly subscription fee to make sure we got the right and serious people to register. Things were going well, and we had early success with a few happily married couples who also started to promote our platform, and sooner than we thought, we started to get reasonable traffic and subscribers on the page. However, the income was not up to satisfaction considering the time we spent on screening or scanning the candidates, ensuring the site was not misleading. All this took up a lot of time. Besides, the management was not keen to promote the website, hire new people or upgrade the site, even though I always felt it had huge potential. I expressed the same to them, even proposing to them that we go global. With my limited knowledge of IT skills, I was not able to take over the whole project independently. I allowed the project to run and saw it dying a slow death over time.

But now I had a taste of running a business, and my confidence grew along with my morale. At that particular time, the trend of nail art and nail extension had just started booming, and I got attracted to this innovation in the beauty industry. In Egypt, this line was quite expensive and not affordable to all. I could only think of one person who could be my best partner in this venture at the time. It was my mom. I spoke to her, and she was willing to explore the opportunity along with me. So, during a short vacation in Ukraine, I registered myself as an individual entrepreneur, rented space for business activity, paid for crash courses for my mom, got her certified as a nail artist, and started our operations. That was my first officially registered business set-up that I did by myself, and I felt so proud to finally have my very first 100% owned company.

My mom was taking care of the business single-handedly, with daily operations and requirements, right from servicing the clients to accounting. I was in charge of all government requirements and approvals, investment and development of the company, operational expenses, etc. The clients were coming through friends and recommendations, purely by word-of-mouth marketing. Things were going in the right direction. The frequency of my visits to Ukraine increased, and later, I started to learn nail art from my mom.

After a few months in business, my mom started to feel weak and tired. Clients were increasing, and so was work. I could have kept more employees, but we were at a point where we had not even reached break even, and adding more expenses didn't seem a good option. But my mom gave up too soon, complaining her eyes were weak and her health was not supporting this kind of operation. Hearing all this was heartbreaking, as I gave priority to her health over my business. Even though my mom had a lot of passion and enthusiasm at the start, it quickly drained off. She could not continue with the responsibility. I was always traveling to and from Egypt on my fixed income, and I could not afford to dedicate too much time to this project either. I questioned myself as to whether I had the courage to jeopardize my overseas income; even though it was not the best yet, it was still better than what my business in Ukraine was making. So, with much disappointment and a heavy heart, I had to take a call to close the salon even though I needed this extra income to help me complete the business diploma that I had enrolled for.

It felt that l was everywhere and nowhere. I had my studies going, the work in Egypt with the Computer Hardware, plus the struggle with the marriage site, and now also the burden of fees that needed to be paid to complete my diploma. Things were not easy. But, no one was keen or supportive of me regarding the challenges I faced. This taught me that it is always important to work with like-minded people. Time had already been wasted, and my mom was not making the best of the opportunity that was provided to her, but life had to go on. Everyone is not the same; given such an opportunity, I would have focused on my targets and probably worked night and day to meet them. **<u>One cannot aim for the stars with a partner that is afraid of heights!</u>**'

I weighed out all the pros and cons and narrowed it down to a vision focusing on my goals which I wrote down: First, I needed to graduate and get my diploma, then I needed to buy my own car, then focus on buying my own house. All of this, I gave myself a time period of four years, and I intended to be committed to it. My vision was purely based on the wealth and prosperity of my finances. My focus turned to my studies, thereby putting a break in my career growth. Even though I was working with all my commitments, it was more like a 9-to-5 job. All my energies were towards the completion of my diploma, and that required a lot of time and dedication.

The on-line project in Egypt was not very lucrative. There was just enough that I could rely on for fulfilling my commitments towards my education without compromising on my living standard. But there was nothing extra that it could provide me to help build myself to the next level of my vision. I again felt I was moving nowhere, and being in Egypt gave me the sense of being stagnant. Hence, I decided I had to make a choice…a choice possibly to move to another country that would help me grow and develop myself, give me financial stability, security and a better opportunity.

I started to look for options, searching for an ideal destination to give a path to my ambition. After a few evaluations and online searches, with some tips and feedback from friends, I soon knew where I wanted to be. I wrapped up all my business commitments, bid farewell to my employees and business partners, got myself a tourist visa, and paid for my tickets and before long, I was already landing in my chosen destination, the business capital and among the most happening place in the region or probably in the world – The United Arab Emirates. This is where I felt my destiny had brought me, and I believed where my future awaited – the city where dreams come true, the city known for opportunities - **<u>Dubai!</u>**

Chapter 14
The Corporate Career

In May 2006, my plane landed in the UAE. It was not the same country as it is today, with a reputation of being among the fastest-growing economies in the world. Today, it is considered to be one of the most modern countries on the globe. With great hope and big dreams in my eyes, I set foot on its soil.

Back then, things were different. I had managed to rent one room, with shared amenities, in Sharjah as this was all I could afford. Sharjah was a blessing for tens of thousands of new strugglers like me, who came to this country seeking opportunities. The Emirate of Sharjah has been the best option as it is the closest neighbour to Dubai - the business capital of the United Arab Emirates and among the most happening cities on the continent!

Staying in Sharjah had an advantage in terms of saving a lot on living costs in comparison to renting in Dubai. However, an advantage on living costs is always packaged with some struggles. Commuting to and fro was beyond imagination. The traffic, congested roads, crowded public transportation, and limited means of transport were part of the life of an ordinary employee commuting to reach Dubai, especially during work hours. Those days the transport systems were not as efficient, and that made shuttling between Sharjah and Dubai the most challenging exercise. The limitation in public transportation due to a few number of buses which were always overcrowded made me feel claustrophobic and, at times, even breathless in the crowd. Besides the hours-on-end traveling time getting to and from work, if one had a spontaneous plan, the waiting time on the open bus station was nearly thirty to forty minutes, at a near average temperature of plus 40 degree Celsius, it was torture and highly demotivating.

I tried other options, such as carpooling services, to commute. That proved even more challenging than public transport, despite being highly-priced due to demand, it was not worth it. The slow bumper-to-bumper traffic, endless braking, dropping and picking points, and all of such inconveniences made me feel as though I was experiencing a Valdivian earthquake throughout the journey. Everything started to feel so annoying and frustrating... I started to ask myself, what am I doing here?

Yes, it was not easy to convince myself to continue and stay under the ordeal. A countless number of times, I was just a click away from booking my flight back to Ukraine. But the fact that I had left everything to come here to make something of myself, and if so many people could live here under similar conditions and work here to make a living, why couldn't I? I reasoned with myself that I was tougher than ever before... I started to believe in myself more, as I knew I could make things happen. Getting a job in Dubai for a young, tall, blonde lady was never a problem, especially with the advantages of the language skills that I had. Speaking reasonable English, perfect Russian and a bit of Arabic, thanks to my previous work experience in Egypt. But the biggest challenge was to obtain a work visa, as work visas were not easy to obtain, especially for CIS workers in the UAE during those years due to red tape and bureaucratic policies.

It took me almost a year of struggle, assisted with several short-term stay visas, helped by friends or through tourism agencies, working part-time jobs or temporary employment trying to cover my living expenses. Sometimes, it seemed impossible, and I would not even have enough money saved to buy myself a decent meal. But all these challenges did not stop me from improving myself. I thought of enhancing and practicing my language skills to help me get better opportunities. English being the business language of the region, I started buying local newspapers and practicing reading. While trying to enhance my vocabulary and learn new words, I kept improvising on the language, taking every opportunity to enhance my skills, my career, and above all, my income.

Almost a year had passed, and the start of the new summer season nearly broke me down. It seemed, under the circumstances, very difficult for me to continue this struggle. And then it happened. A day came when all my hard work, struggle, and challenges had finally paid off. I was selected by one of the region's largest FMCG companies for a position in sales, and as promised, they provided me with all the official documents and permits required. Finally, a residence work visa was stamped on my passport. I could barely control my feelings, and I remember crying with happiness. It was among the best moments of my life since the time I arrived in the UAE. All this was only possible due to my strong-mindedness and determination towards my goal.

Finally, I had an opportunity, a proper official job in an FMCG career, and I just felt that this was the career I belonged to. My ability to be a quick learner helped me pave the road toward corporate life. I started enhancing and improving myself. I got my driver's license, something that was not only required to help me commute in comfort and convenience (Thank God for that!) but also to help improve my work performance.

It was the beginning of a different world, a new corporate world based on judging performance through means of evaluation and targets, training and discussing market competition, and in-house team performance, among others. My life had changed. I was living a life beyond my expectations and enjoying every bit of it.

Today, when I look back, I wonder what I would have done if I had broken down and given up had this opportunity not knocked at my door. The struggle was hard, more than averagely challenging, and it took away every bit of my energy and made me run out of patience. It cost me every single bit of determination that I had to finally get myself an opportunity in this land known as the Land of Opportunities, teaching me – **'The struggle is never about hearing an opportunity knock. It is all about being patient till one finds the door it knocks at.'**

During the period of my tenure in my first corporate job, my way of dealing with people changed drastically. I started to read a lot of business books, trying to enrich my vocabulary, enhance my communication skills, and evaluate all the nitty-gritty of how people were getting promoted. Being inquisitive by nature, a habit that has always made me curious to find out in detail how things work, a habit that has always helped me to know better, I came to realize that success is not always dependent on one's performance alone. It is also dependent on the fact of whom you know and what you know that strongly applies in such circumstances. How one can build a relationship and how one can promote oneself to achieve the desired targets is crucial in this cruel, challenging world of corporates. It is always about your connection, your skills, how you manage things, how you sugarcoat things, and how you can present your talents towards your enhancement is all that matters.

It didn't take me long to blend and understand the structure. I soon started to advance in my approach, making sure my ideas were heard by the right people, grabbing all opportunities, and speaking at conferences and team meetings. Soon enough, I got spotted by one of the multinational companies that we were distributors of in the region. Not wasting a moment, I took up the opportunity, a huge break in my career. Now, I was working for a globally recognized multinational company—a milestone of achievement!

In terms of my personal assessment, this would be a different world, but to my surprise, the struggle I faced was, in a lot of ways, very similar and even much more brutal. It was like being upgraded to the next level of the game. It seemed to be a constant fight, a fight to survive, a rat race to compete, an endless challenge without which one could not proceed further. In this survival of the fittest, one had to be faster, stronger, more focused, and of a level that was way ahead of anything that could be imagined unless the person had prior experience of it. The most important leader is the one who promotes oneself and expresses one's every single achievement with enhancement. The rule was: Always be visible in front of the management, be noticed, and be alert, be ready, be at your very best. The best way to do so was to have discussions, and chats with your seniors, know your aims and targets, be intensive, and be dedicated towards your goals.

I realized soon that getting ahead was all about you and a lot of how you present yourself to your seniors. To help your career to zoom with speed, performance meant an urge to self-growth. It means you do it for yourself or get ready to be walked over by the mob. I have always been good at enhancing my skills and realized that marketing myself was not too difficult. Selling a world-renounced brand is far less challenging than marketing oneself. Achieving my targets in sales was not much of a challenge as I had the support and the backing of a trusted brand, a brand known in the world for decades. Plus, my persistence and efforts with the skill set to think beyond the ordinary helped me reach my sales targets with ease. I was not shy to share new ideas and was good at presenting them with full confidence, strongly and convincingly. All was possible because I believed in myself, in my concepts, and had a powerful point of view about it. Thus, I was doing very well for myself, growing at a fast pace in my career.

Well, as they say, what comes fast doesn't last. It is not only your skill set or your talent that is enough, but one also need to be vigilant while for working for the corporates. I learnt that the faster you grow, the harder you fall if you are not cautious. My over-enthusiasm in providing new ideas and concepts was used by others for their own interest. This was exactly what happened, as my seniors took my proven ideas and presented them as their own to the higher management taking all the credit, and I was deprived of what I had worked for and so rightly deserved. I was very naïve, and perhaps it took me a lot of time to understand the crude reality.

Multinational corporates are a great experience as long as you are dedicated and focused. But it tends to give you a horse vision; it wants you to live, breathe, eat, and drink more like being a frog in the well. Of course, that, too, has its benefits for people who can adjust, learn and move forward. So I was grooming and growing with the culture and, in a lot of ways, starting to feel the comfort zone during my career by unquestionably accepting the good and the evil of things. Timely growth, promotions, and appreciation, though not for all your achievements, as a lot of it gets filtered, at that moment all seemed to be manageable as long as I progressed in my career.

I was happy and in my comfort zone, accepting all the pros and cons and living a robotic corporate lifestyle, working with all my devotion for a multi-national company and also simultaneously growing in my personal life. I was blessed with a baby boy, and he resembled so much to my late father, so his birth was among the most overwhelming moments of my life. Things were all perfectly fine after my first maternity leave when I joined the company. I was officially assigned a new boss. I was excited to work with her as I felt, being a woman, she would understand me better both as a career woman and a nursing mom. What more could I have asked for? Life was such a blessing. But all that glitters is not gold, and maybe God had better plans.

To start with, I respected my new boss, a single mother taking care of her child, her courage and capabilities and for being way more experienced with the corporate structure and how it functioned. I was already a fan and was looking up to her as my mentor to help me grow, anticipating new learning and further development of myself. However, the human mind works in mysterious ways, and a lot of times, people tend to forget their own blessings and focus on other individuals, comparing themselves to them and in the way of competing with them, perhaps, just to prove their own competency. It was not hard to understand right from the start that she had different views about me. Perhaps, she envied my achievements and success at a young age; I had climbed up my career ladder, growing consistently in my professional life and managing a stable personal life.

It is not uncommon to see people mix their personal life with their professional ones, and in this case, she made it very obvious. She started commenting on my looks, mocking me on silly things like the way I carried myself, how I talked and walked, and what I wore, making me conscious of everything I was doing. She dug out the history and found out about my professional achievements, my appreciation certificates and awards that I had received from the company, connecting them to my personality and looks instead of associating them with my hard work and efforts that were so genuinely earned. She would taunt me at any and every opportunity she got, showing me down in front of my colleagues and mocking me during group meetings. She would even throw inappropriate sarcastic comments, tarnishing my respectful reputation, even to the extent of being sarcastic in accusing me of possibly having questionable relations with my colleague. I had no idea why she was so inappropriate and unprofessional towards me, except she was jealous!

Maybe my achievements seemed far-fetched to her, and she could not accept that I managed to advance at a fast pace in such a short time, but it was not something that just fell into my lap. I had worked very hard, smart, and creatively to reach this far at that pace, taking chances, performing under timeline pressures with all my dedication, and achieving targets. Opening new possibilities with reputed customers in the region, creating new ideas, and being persistent in trying them out, they were overruled, or many a time, not even understood initially. I strived to be convincing, committing, and obtaining my goals purely through my dedication, creating challenges for myself, and meeting them. It was not my looks or glamor that got me where I was. Her petty thinking and the constant pressure affected my health severely. Being a nursing mother and going through psychological and hormonal changes, as every woman does, I was timid and felt vulnerable, weak, and broken. I was on the edge of falling into depression, and with all this pressure, I felt tortured in the same office that I used to look forward to going to every morning, and now it felt like being in a concentration camp. I was so much under stress that my body stopped lactating in the first couple of months, and I had no choice but to feed my baby with formula milk much before his weaning time. This was among the worst nightmares that a mother could experience, and even today, when I recall those days, I get tremors and can't control my emotions.

I learnt from her how crazy the corporate world can really be, and for me, it was a severe lesson. Planned exploitation, late hours at work, discouragement despite prominent results, numerous attempts, and threats of termination, insulting, and criticizing: All this took me out of my comfort zone and encouraged me to re-think my way forward. I started looking for other possibilities, but this time I was certain I did not want a job as a sales executive. I was aiming higher. I started looking for opportunities where I could be exposed to various markets, travel and experience different work cultures, and my search was constant and consistent. I was assiduously determined to find that kind of job. Until then, I would not rest. I am a firm believer that if you ask the universe what you want, with all you have, the universe helps you with it, and that was exactly what happened after nearly 18 months of persistent searching. I was offered a job by another leading MNC that appointed me as a regional food service manager for the entire Middle East region.

Everything has its phases, and today, when I think of it, I am grateful for the experience. Yet, some things hurt so deeply that they are difficult to forget. I guess it was required to wake me up, but going through it during that moment veritably shook off the ground below me. Probably, if it had not been so hard, it may not have taken me out of my comfort zone and may not have helped me be where I am today.

A new challenge, new working environment, new line of products, better pay, better position: I could not have asked for more. I had taken a big leap in my career, and I was so looking forward to it. Even though it was hard to forget what I had gone through, I still managed to get the strength to pardon her behavior and move on with my professional life. Thanking the Universe for this opportunity, I was now looking at a much better prospect.

Stepping into the new horizon! It did not take me time to recover from my past. Based on my professional background, backed with good experience, I already knew how things work. Holding an 'excellence in performance' certificate from my previous company made me confident, determined and committed. My positivity was at a new high, and the feeling of being resurrected made me feel alive again. Moving to bigger and better assignments of work, with new challenges and new learnings, along with one of the world's market leaders in dairy, not only gave me relief but also sparked enthusiasm back into my life!

My job consisted of a lot of new learning, such as packaging requirements, labeling details, branding, export documentation norms, and many more such things. It turned out to be an ocean of new thrilling experiences. Regular travel to manufacturing facilities, seeing new countries, working on new projects and products, enhancing my know-how... Everything was so exciting! I became a frequent flyer, getting lounge card access to international destinations. Maybe it might sound a little childish, but when one gets the privilege for the first time, one tends to feel as ecstatic as a small kid till one grows out of it. It was not just the comfort and privilege of using the lounge or getting priorities as a frequent flyer that excited me, but the accompanying lifestyle that fascinated me the most.

The new job was a dream come true, but it came with a lot of responsibilities, such as analyzing markets, shortlisting and appointing distributors based on their distribution strengths, developing a new range of products, learning the psychology of different markets, understanding the taste preference, commercializing, and launching. It was a lot of work, but the thrill of doing it was even more exciting, especially when you saw and analyzed your own performance through the results and profits that you generated for the company was like the icing on the cake, keeping me motivated and helping me grow.

My income grew, my career grew, my exposure grew, and my know-how grew, but what grew the most along with all that was also my desire to have my very own business one day. This was something that I could never grow out of. I knew that one day I shall, but until then, I had to plan and manage my investments for my future business. I started planning. Life had taught me the hard way not to keep all eggs in one basket, so I started to look into different options, such as National bonds, long-term fixed deposits, properties, and gold. Keeping my savings in different pockets helped me stay at peace, insuring periodic consistent and secure growth of my investments with calculated risks.

However, all this never stopped me from investing in myself. Yes, I continued advancing in my education. I got enrolled in an MBA for distance learning. Later I obtained a diploma in genetic engineering which also helped me enhance my skills and knowledge of production in the dairy industry, deepening my technical know-how of processing and manufacturing various dairy derivatives.

During the time when I was working for the FMCG consumer industry and building my professional network to help promote my business, one of my clients asked me if I could source and supply them sunflower oil, knowing well that I was from Ukraine, a country known to be among the largest producers of helianthus oil in the world. Initially, just to support them, I started to ask my contacts back home to help me connect with the right suppliers or manufacturers of sunflower oil for supplies to the Middle East markets. While doing so, I got more curious and started to understand the trade of this highly commercial commodity, studying the possibility of trading in it. I started doing a feasibility study, trying to understand if this could be a viable future business and perhaps support to help me kick start my very own trading establishment.

Chapter 15
My Path to Becoming an
Entrepreneur!

It is not only about feasibility. A start-up needs much more than just funding and planning. Creating the company, getting it registered, and making it a legal entity are some of the formalities needed to be completed. I was not ready to get into it as I already had my hands full with my present professional commitments. Even though it would be a milestone towards my desire to have my own business, it was a commitment I was not ready to get into.

Then, one day, during a short holiday in Ukraine, I ran into an old friend. I have known him as a trader since my days of working for the bank. While catching up on things, I shared my thoughts with him, keeping in mind the Sunflower Oil sourcing, which one of my clients was still looking for a reliable source. To my surprise, he encouraged me to start a company in partnership with him in Ukraine. He was trading mainly with walnuts and sunflower oil, and he convinced me that he had a lot of know-how about the trade and that with the right partner and connectivity in the Middle East, he could support the business and make it worth the effort. I was convinced not only because I felt he had the experience of how to do the business but also because of the fact that these products are not directly related or competing with the dairy industry that I was working and representing. The business would remain in Ukraine and would not be a hindrance. These facts made me feel ethical towards my duties and also safe under the law. However, I made it clear to him that I would not be able to dedicate much time to the project, at which he assured me that all I had to do was to get him connected with the client, and he would do the rest. This suggestion from him added fuel to the fire of my desire to own my own business, and I agreed to be a part of it.

All documents and arrangements were quickly processed. My partner was an expert at it since he had years of experience in doing business. We opened an overseas bank account as it was the cheapest option, especially when you would deal in foreign currency. As we had only planned to do export, so it was most convenient. He did an impressive job quickly and promptly. Even though I had some savings, I still preferred to arrange funds through one of the banks in UAE; this way, I arranged financing of the initial capital as my personal loan. The start of this new partnership seemed very systematic, with responsibilities shared on the basis of the capabilities and strengths of each partner.

As mentioned, I still had my job and launching this company made me in a manner more conscious and responsible towards my commitments. I started to put more effort into the progress of sales, marketing and business development. My distribution was growing, and so were the sales, achieving record targets with distribution spread across 12 countries around the MENA region. My performance was accelerating, and the management granted me a lot of flexibility and trust in operations. Hence, I could not fail them. Furthermore, I loved what I was doing; it was motivating, with healthy, fruitful growth, as also an outcome of my hard work and efforts. The loyalty and commitment towards the company were total.

However, I did my part as a partner towards my own business, supporting my partner both with funds and also connecting him to potential partners in the regions I was working with, but as agreed between us, I was not getting involved in operations, something I had made clear right from the start. But my curious self could not hold to learn and understand my partner's methods of working whenever possible, I was asking him for details and learning new things from him as a business owner…things like how to operate a foreign bank account, purchase goods from a third party, shipping of goods to various destinations, basic trading, and re-exporting of goods, sometimes acting as an agent and at times just as a broker. It was complicated at times, but I grasped it fast!

As my job responsibilities grew, so did my trust in my partner. I started to focus more on my career, leaving all business responsibilities in the reliable hands of my partner. Anytime he needed funds, I would either send through my savings or take additional personal loans, ensuring he was not short of it, as commodity business requires huge capital. I always believed that you should treat others the way you want to be treated, and I started supporting my partner without an ounce of doubt, expecting him to use the funds wisely and for the benefit of the business with total trust and good faith. Gradually, all operations were handed over to my partner, including access to banking services. The frequency of my travels to Ukraine was limited as my travel and work commitments for my job were always on priority; this did not allow me to interfere with my own business operations. I was under the impression that I had invested in the business with experienced hands that seemed to be committed towards the task. What could possibly go wrong? It was not long before when the orders started to come in, and the business started to gain momentum; I was happy things were moving great. I felt my investment was safe and I could blindly rely on my responsible partner.

One Saturday afternoon, as I was relaxing with my family, I got a call from one of my referred clients. He had confirmed an order with my partner after taking assurance from me and had sent advance payment for the shipment, but it had been over a month since my partner had updated him on the progress of his order. This came as a surprise to me, and I started to investigate and question my partner about the order. He gave me an explanation that was not up to my satisfaction. I started to check, questioning him and expecting detailed answers. Upon digging deep, it came to my notice that reports of company transactions were not available. There were false entries in account books and issues with export documents, labels and pricing. Orders of clients were pending, and my partner was so relaxed, but it was my reputation that was at stake. Most of the clients had started business with my partner based on my guarantee. I was in a panic situation and stayed endlessly on calls with my partner to understand what had gone wrong.

My partner, who seemed overconfident about his source of purchase, made a deal through a middleman even though he had direct access to the factory. When questioned, he claimed he got a better deal from him. The middleman, after receiving payment from us for the goods, suddenly started to delay the shipment. I got deeply involved to help sort the issue. Through my limited yet reliable contacts and connections, after nearly three months, we managed to retrieve the funds. As soon as we got the funds, we paid the factory for processing the pending orders that we had. I could save face with the clients, and only because of the relationship of trust they shared with me did they remain patient. Later, I found that my partner had also made another deal with a shipment of walnuts and one of our walnut containers, which was fully paid for, got stolen in the port, is what I was told. Just to save a few dollars, he had not insured the container. All of a sudden, everything I had paid to build this company was gone. To date, we have not managed to get a single dollar in claims for the stolen container, and I have lost all hope that we ever will.

These episodes exhausted me. I had to freeze all operations of the company for almost three months to sort out the issues, leading to the slow death of both my partnership and the company. It was a mistake to trust someone so blindly and give the responsibility of all my funds into the hands of a person who never valued it just because it came easy to him. Legally, he was not bound to any financial obligations. This was realized during the crisis, and I had signed all documents purely based on trust. From the very start, I had missed the point. I had not clearly defined the terms and conditions, plus the responsibilities of each partner.

The only thing I could take away from the experience was the knowledge and the learning of how the game was played in the commodity trade. This connected me with some very strong companies and helped me understand the market requirements. Now more than ever before, I knew how it was done. I believe this exposure, experience and the knowledge I gained under these circumstances, no university in the world could have taught me. I learnt a lot through these events, and taking this as a positive yield from the episode, I moved on with the hope that perhaps one day, I shall get it right! Taking the good from it and putting the rest behind me, I got back into my routine job. All this pressure, coupled with the crisis of my own company, made me exhausted. But, I never ignored or compromised with my duties and always did my job with complete dedication and responsibility. Plus, I was getting ready to bring my daughter into this amazing world. I did not want to carry grievances; I wanted peace, love, and care to help develop my baby fetus, and with all positivity, I started focusing on my job and my personal development.

Well, all things have a bright side to them and happen for the right reasons. My natural resilience helped me overcome the crises and also taught me to assess people and understand them better. Taking the opportunity of my maternity leave that was due soon, I planned to further continue my studies and registered myself for a Master's Degree in Genetics.

Yes, even though business has always been my passion, I have this zeal for human DNA. I have been curious to understand the human aging process and how our DNAs have mutated and evolved over millions of years. Nature's technology is a tiny strip that is a key to our existence, and that helps us live and survive through the sands of time. Deep inside, this has always fascinated me. Thus, I got myself registered for the courses that triggered my true fascination and hence enrolled to study genetics

I always believe in planning, and with this incident, I hit a bull's eye! My second child's arrival was perfectly synchronized with my admission to the university so that during maternity leave, I could focus on my studies. Since I was still a corporate employee, I made sure my work stress did not allow me to get affected during my second pregnancy. Even though it was not the same company and not the same boss, I had developed a phobia and didn't want to take any chances. As planned, things fell perfectly into place. And all through my maternity, I dedicated myself to studying. Submitting my thesis, doing research, and reading a lot.

Soon the day came, and I was blessed with a baby girl so cute as though the heavens had opened to bless her to me. After my pregnancy, I was back at work, and things were different. During my break, the top management had changed and taking advantage of this changeover, one of my subordinates, whom I had hired as my assistant, played her corporate games during my absence. But getting back into the game felt so tiresome. It was a never-ending exhausting phenomenon. But this time, I was not weak like the last, and my confidence level was much higher. With a reputation I had earned over the years, it took me just a couple of calls, and I moved, taking up another opportunity with yet another MNC, this time in a different role; I was assigned to develop the UAE regional markets something that I knew I could with least stress.

Yet, once I started my new venture, it felt like I had to go back to square one. Again it was the same…blending with new working culture, learning, explaining, developing… This made me think: "Is this what I really want?" Working a full-time job under tremendous pressure, keep proving myself, protecting my position, always alert, and always insecure no matter how confident and knowledgeable one may be; being a full-time mother of two, working hard to ensure my child is at school on time while the other is taken care of at home when you are away; reaching office on the dot, your meetings and your targets, proving your achievements: Was this all I wanted? I was already drained by this hectic and monotonous life, a life that gave me a livelihood at a very high cost. But I still continued, allowing myself to get tangled more and more into the web of the corporate world.

One day, my five-year-old son got admitted to the hospital due to a bacterial infection, and his temperature was not coming down. I asked my regional director for an emergency off, to which he replied – "You are not sick, your son is. Adjust the day off against your annual leave, as we can't give you any humanitarian days off." It was not the matter of an off that I reacted to, but the manner the message was given, so abrupt and merciless and that too, at a time when I was shaken up due to my son's condition.

I guess, at times, one needs a push to take the plunge! Being at the peak of my career, honest, hardworking, ethical, a sincere worker generating results for the companies, I had worked thanklessly, putting all my genuine efforts into my job. Thus the kind of attitude shown made me quiver…rather, let's just say it woke me up from my somnambulism. Soon after this realization, I put in my papers and moved out of the ruthless set-up of corporate life.

I was quick to register my company INAS EXIM LLC as an independent unit driven by women. My childhood classmate, who was working with my ex-partner as a customer service specialist, joined me as the export manager to handle my operations in Ukraine. This time the bank account and funds were under my control, and I took sole responsibility for being the decision-maker for my own company.

"INAS EXIM LLC—International Network for Achievable Solutions. What made us different was that we are not just another trading company but act as partners with our clients to find the right key to success. Providing the right products at a fair cost paving the road to growth by ensuring Easy, Profitable and Sustainable answers to any business. We understand, evaluate, and analyze our customers' needs to help create a win-win solution. Our team of experts and networking can help develop specialized and customized products…" Wow! I can go on and on about my company. The excitement is never-ending and always ecstatic!!

What looks easy was not achieved overnight. Today I look back and thank all the people who did me a favour, for without them, I would never have woken up and planned my exit to start on my very own. I would also like to thank myself for not breaking down. No matter how much I got twisted, bent, and stretched, my resilience helped me to bounce back. I never stopped believing in myself; I never doubted my strength, and this helped me build myself bigger and stronger.

Chapter 16
Building Resilience

Establishing and taking your first step towards a startup in business is not just a matter of simple registration of the legal entity and getting a license to trade. You have to be prepared for new horizons and new challenges. It is how to manage different situations and cope with the stress level that you will experience.

Allow me to review this with a simple example. Let's say you are in a space shuttle on a mission. Why are you there? Let us just say the mission is to collect moon rock samples. Then comes the vision – Why do you need the rock samples from the moon? You may answer: To try possible options for developing oxygen levels and water retention to cultivate agriculture on the moon. And now, the most important query: What do you depend on? The space shuttle is the only means of survival and way back. So, in this case, the space shuttle acts like your resilience. No matter what, you will always try to ensure that your space shuttle is in perfect condition technically.

You get trained physically according to space travel medics; you manage to pass strict exams to get permission for the travel. It is hard. Sometimes it seems impossible. It needs a lot of persistence fighting with your 'can'ts' and changing them to 'cans'. You have to understand mentally that it is not easy to be enclosed in space under stress, all alone, surrounded by no one; you can breathe only within the limitation of space provided inside the spacecraft. The nutrition programs adjust your daily food intake in extreme conditions, which is different from normal eating habits, and you have to exercise a lot to be physically strong. You've been taught and trained on all the technical approaches towards your mission, and you get a space shuttle to help you live and survive in extreme environmental conditions.

Have you thought about the spacecraft itself? Let's look at it too; endless numbers of engineers worked round the clock to assemble the shuttle. How many mistakes occurred while trying to ensure its improved performance each time? For sure, there was a lot of learning, repeated trials, and persistence, but all those people never gave up and used all their experiences, knowledge, and skills collectively to get a space shuttle built for the condition it should be used, ensuring its performance even under extreme challenges. After all that, only your trust is in the spacecraft and your faith in yourself, your skills, your attitude, and your conviction to take up a challenge.

Now let's connect the above with the practical life of an entrepreneur since a similar concept applies to the process of establishing your business. You have your mission and your vision; you plan for it and prepare yourself physically and mentally for it. Your experiences and challenges are the engineers that build your resilience (spacecraft). No matter what your circumstances are, you must adjust and manage to keep your spacecraft in perfect condition and continue to move on.

As an entrepreneur, one has to be emotionally prepared for any kind of distraction and keep the focus on solutions, not to sulk but excel beyond. One has to develop strength before starting any business venture and the feeling to fight any situation that comes, keeping your resilience craft always at its best. You will fall; you will break down, but you will come back because no matter what happens, the spacecraft (resilience) that you have, was built with years of detailed engineering (experiences) by you.

Some of my experiences are worth sharing in order to understand how it was engineered to help build my resilience. At the time when I was at the peak of my employment career working for a multinational company, I had an assistant who was employed/hired by me. While interviewing her, I found her to be very innocent, sharing her struggle with her present work and how she would, if given the opportunity, perform with our multinational organization. I liked her frankness and innocence-like approach. It made me feel I could mould her into an excellent team member and help her grow. I began taking extra efforts to help ensure the vacancy was filled by her by guiding her step by step through all her interviews, giving her instructions about what she had to say, explaining the culture of the company and what would help her get the position until she finally made it and got the job as my assistant.

As a team leader, I always kept investing in my team, and for her, my efforts were more persistent, continuously helping to improve her by signing her up for training and seminars, sharing my experiences, giving her more responsibilities to handle, and opening new doors for her to travel to international markets, study products, visit factories, and attend meetings with overseas clients. I felt happy as she was growing by leaps and bounds and developing herself well. I had no one to mould me and had a tough learning journey, struggling through every step, but I had laid it down for her.

After some time, my line manager, to whom I was directly reporting, had a change in career and moved to a different company for better opportunities during the time I was pregnant with my second child. But my relationship with my line manager was very strong, and we worked well together. Even after he moved away, we were always in touch, and he had a soft corner for me, especially when I was going through my pregnancy. He used to praise me for my skills in managing so much work pressure, handling multi countries, and traveling, and now he had to leave. In multinationals, changes in senior positions are always stressful due to new ideas, new concepts, and new ways of thinking, as also new challenges.

An overseas recruit from the global head office temporarily filled his position. I being so well experienced and well synchronized with the post, was expecting career growth and a climb up the ladder, and the temporary replacement gave me hope. Maybe, there would be a change after my maternity leave, perhaps. Thus keeping my morale high, as soon as the new manager took charge, he changed the company insurance policy, opting for cheaper insurance and cutting my maternity benefits, providing me with peanuts for maternity. He wanted to show profits for the company by cutting corners. It got me worried, stressed and tensed with all sorts of thoughts that disturbed me, mainly due to my pregnancy, and it was hard to keep in check.

During pregnancy, emotions get the better of you. I felt that all my hard work and efforts for the company were not appreciated. I wondered how the head-office could allow this to happen. This was disrespectful to my child and me and against human rights. It was a time when I could not hold back my emotions. I kept reminding myself I was overreacting due to my physical condition. As mentioned in my previous chapter, during this time, I had also binned my overseas business investment just to ensure a healthy second pregnancy. This added a lot of extra pressure, but I somehow managed to keep my calm.

On the face of it, my new line manager gave me a lot of importance. He treated me with respect, making me feel like an essential part of the company. We used to have regular meetings along with the team to discuss the future and the plans to restructure my department and help progress. Taking my ideas on the upcoming projects and, at what stage they stood, trying to understand the next phase of things that needed to be done, my clients were all handed over to my assistant, and she was asked to keep the ball rolling and was asked to train her and during the period allow her to handle everything with little or no interference so she can get acquainted with my duties before I availed my maternity leave. I felt a bit suspicious about this call; I was always involved with the department, even when I was on annual leave in the past. I felt there was something fishy. After all, I was the most experienced and was handling 12 markets. It had never been easy; plus, my assistant was not qualified or experienced to manage the whole operation single-handedly. But again, I thought I was overthinking. All importance and attention were given to me to help provide extra information about things, and I being a professional and a dedicated worker, did my best to hand over all details to my assistant, helping her understand even the minor elements of the operation.

Finally, the day before my maternity leave, I got shocking news. My line manager position would now be permanently taken over by the new recruit, and my assistant would directly report to him until I was back. I, too, was to work under his administration upon return, even though he had no idea about the region. I, therefore, went on leave, a lot frustrated and feeling deprived. It was like a psychological tremor at that stage of my pregnancy. But I managed to keep my mind focused on my pregnancy and felt that other things could be dealt with later. I knew my life was going to change, but how? I had no clue; even though the anxiety was building up within me, I had a million questions thinking of what would happen upon my return. What are the plans of the company? Yet, I still kept my nerve.

During my maternity leave, I kept chatting with my assistant on a regular basis, making sure things were going fine. I slowly started to notice that she had a big admiration for the new boss, despite the fact that the sales reports that I was being copied on showed that the department was not performing and they were not able to meet the targets. Making a note of things, yet not reacting, I just kept my focus on both my pregnancy and my Genetics Studies until that special day arrived, and my delivery was splendid, blessed with the cutest baby girl I had ever seen. I forgot all my sorrows and issues, and once again, God blessed me to bring another soul to this beautiful world. I was more relaxed, more living the moment, busy changing diapers, waiting to see her first smile, enjoying every minute of it!

Time flies faster than one can imagine; I was heading back to Dubai to resume my duties. On the first day at work, I had butterflies in my stomach. My assistant had hardly been in touch with me for almost a month, and the day I walked into the office, it did not take me time to understand why. She and my line manager had all things set for themselves. He had changed the reporting, and she had to report to him directly. My best-developed markets were given permanently to her to handle. She was personally driving him around. They were planning business trips and taking extra days for every destination and many such things. It felt like it was all going well for them, a set market that I had worked so hard for, and taking the credit and enjoying the fruits of it.

It all happened sooner than I could imagine, and I was put in a corner, asked to prove myself, and eventually, in an unjust manner (in my opinion), they teamed up to ask me to leave. I was prepared and knew my legal rights. UAE law is fair and balanced. It did take me time, but eventually, it favoured me and helped me get my deserved rights. I was happy to move out of a company that did not appreciate the efforts that were so genuinely and sincerely put in by me to help achieve new heights. I felt deceived and tricked, but my resilience helped me recover and move forward. All I wanted now was to start my mission to reach my vision in my spacecraft.

To develop your resilience, you should deeply understand yourself, analyze what kind of difficult situations you've been going through, and how you react. People are not always as they seem, and when I was new in the business, my ex-Line Manager, who was also a close friend, opted to support me. It was a great feeling to know someone was standing with me to help me grow, someone who has morally helped and supported me over the years, a genuine well-wisher. I was new at trading and started to work on the project with him, trying to export cheese to his client through his private company. We arranged samples, did trials, and negotiated prices till, finally, the first container was successfully confirmed and sold.

After the first deal was completed, I was on top of the world. I trusted it would continue to be the same, and he being a known personality in the industry, plus my ex-colleague with a history of working together, I permitted myself not to be involved in all shipments personally. I allowed him to deal with my source in Ukraine to continue supplies and exports in the same manner as agreed.

Based purely on blind trust, all transactions were approved by me. I was transparent enough to reveal my sources and contacts, expecting that he would be ethical in his dealing and everything would continue the same way. After a few months, I realized things were not moving as they were expected to, and upon investigating, I was shocked to know that he had shipped over a dozen containers acting on my behalf using my approvals, bypassing me. To date, he still denies it even though all the evidence proves otherwise. Over and above that, he dared to quote me an indecent proposal when I visited his office, acting naïve about his backstabbing act on me. It made me understand how people can be; it was unexpected, and all his support to me was not as a friend but to take undue advantage of me, to get my contacts and also his wrong intentions for me; these seemed to be his ultimate targets.

At first, I thought I had lost a friend, the trust, and the money, but instead of grumbling, I was quick to understand it was not worth it. I realized it wasn't me who had lost a friend and trust, but he. Money was a short-term gain, but he lost a friend that could trust him, and all the money in the world would not be able to buy that for him. I stopped all business transactions with him. Later, when he found out that I knew about his unethical act, he stopped all his communication with me. He lost a friend, a partner and, above all, his credibility. He did utilize the opportunity provided in the best possible way just for short-term gain. Over that, he still had the arrogance to make a personal pass at me. This experience taught me a lot. By losing a few thousand dollars on these deals, I learnt and prevented what could have been a much bigger loss had I continued trusting and doing business with him. Being grateful for this experience, my resilience again kicked in, reminding me about my ultimate goal.

Yes, it was a mistake to trust by sharing all my sources, but I still believe that trust exists between the right business partners; one grows together for bigger achievements. I learnt to keep and retain information in the best possible manner to protect my business interests and only disclose what I am ready to share. People are not always as they show themselves to be. It did hurt me, but I took it as an example of how I managed the situation where I was cheated and unfairly treated. Whatever I extracted from this learning, I implemented it in my future operations, giving priority to protecting and safeguarding my business information.

Do not torture yourself by trying to regret the moments of failure. It is better to analyze the situation and in the best possible manner to solve the issue. Never let the stress take advantage of you, and do not overthink. If you need help, make sure to ask, but choose the right people. You have to adapt fast to risks and be proactive in finding solutions.

Always remember, people pretend to be professionals unless put to the test and one would see wolves in sheep's clothing. The best way to learn about a person is by giving them power and seeing whether they respect it and use it rightly or go beyond their capacity to abuse it no matter how professional they are or pretend to be. Placing your trust in the right hands is an important rule that must always be followed.

So, now if I am in space and have an oxygen leakage issue with the shuttle, I shall not look to trust an architect specialized in designing the shuttle but more to the engineer who can help me solve my oxygen issue with quicker solutions and proper repairs. Above all, I shall trust my instincts to be my best guide because there is nothing above self-trust, and without my courage, this journey would never have taken place in the first place!

The engineer that helps me when I run out of oxygen in my spacecraft is Passion!

Chapter 17
Passion

I believe that the best fuel in one's life is passion. Passion is the power that helps you work towards your dreams. Persistence is important at work and may bring you discipline, certain admiration, and work satisfaction, but passion is not about your routine, work, or how you handle things. It is about your desire, your devotion, and your feelings towards what you want. It is what gives you the drive. Disregard if your aim seems to be unachievable at a certain stage of life or not, but your passion gives you the intuition that you shall achieve it. Don't forget to look back at times to see how far you have come, but never get disappointed if your progress has been slow. Slow progress is far better than no progress. Keep your aims higher, and do not underestimate yourself.

As a young girl with a passion for discovering myself as a holistic person, I was always curious, asking myself, what is the purpose of me? Who am I? Who are we? What is the meaning of our existence? What is the purpose of life?... Trying to understand the phenomenon: How, miraculously, a child comes to the world, the first cry of breath, the scare of stepping into a new living atmosphere…the life presented from the other side, coming out of the water to the surface of the undiscovered ambiance of unknown feelings, the feeling towards the difference in the temperature, the fear of newness and the uncertainty when you are lifted, washed, wrapped in a warm cloth and carried into the arms of someone you have already known. Then the first soft and warm connection with the mother's skin, the first movement of the lips, trying to suck the first sip of breast milk... and the cry goes off after being cuddled and feeling secure. Life is not to look for purpose but to live it, to *create* your purpose from it.

I was questioning how we are welcomed into this world, and we will all continue to adapt, adjust, learn, discover, make mistakes, fall, stand up again, and move on, further and further towards our destinies. The path is measured by the number of years, starting with the date and time mentioned on a strip of paper tied around your tiny little legs by the hospital staff; one has to grow to learn how precious life is and enjoy even the last breath of air that enters your lungs. If the purpose of life is the same for us, then why do each one of us have a different time to live, why are we getting old, and why does everyone and everything end?

As a young child, I often kept thinking about these things during moments with my inner self, at times talking to interesting people, also freaking them out with my curiosity. I grew up with this curiosity of trying to understand and find answers. Hence, I developed a passion for genetics. But, due to the country's political and economic status, the education system was still new and needed a lot of improvement. Getting into the field of Genetics at that state was unaffordable and would have required overseas transfer after a point. My family or I couldn't have supported me with my passion. Left with limited choices, I chose to pursue my higher education in business and made a promise to myself that one day, I would pursue my education in Genetics by myself. Focused on my future, I progressed forward on the life path that was destined for me.

I developed a new desire to go beyond the borders of my country, discover the world, and find ways of stable and reasonable income to help grow myself, both professionally and financially, so I can follow my suppressed passion and my secret desire to discover human creation through Genetics. To help fuel my desire, I saw potential in choosing the line of international business as a source of future development and with the possibility that one day, I shall have my own international company and shall pursue my passion.

What has inspired me is that from childhood, I had seen some of my family friends who were working overseas being better off and respected by society. So, I had it in my mind that the source of better income could be possible through the international channel. This would help bridge the economic gap and fulfill my desire to study Genetics to help discover the code of life; understand the process of aging, and perhaps find the Philosopher's Stone ☺

I do not regret deviating from my strategy and looking into a practical way of handling myself at that particular moment when life had left me with few choices. I took a call and made my decision. My passion led me to a different angle of success, and I became an entrepreneur. With stability, I found the courage and again started to follow my passion. The path taken to be an entrepreneur was with a single purpose. However, it helped me achieve more than I had aimed for. I got into a recognized University to finally pursue BIO learning. I am proud to say that I managed to qualify in Genetics and am planning to further practice on a more advanced level.

While pursuing my studies, I've been asked many times: Why and how will it bring value to my business? I just smile back at them and say –**"This was the purpose that helped me create my destiny!"** Many do not understand what I mean.

My passion for studying Genetics led me to build my trading company. It was not something I planned or aimed for, but I am proud of my achievements. I could have sat down and regretted that life is not fair. I could have just accepted the fact that I could not afford to pursue my passion, and I could have blamed the circumstances, but instead, I chose not to. I chose to face it, fight it, go with the flow, and yet be focused on my target until I achieved it!

At the time when I was enrolling for my exams at the university, no one around me, neither my friends nor family, understood why I needed to do this. It was just a long-term project of the young girl born under the communist regime of the USSR who was so passionate about the mystery of human genetics…so simple, and there was nothing more to it!

After my graduation, I decided not to pursue a career as a scientist and instead focused on building my own business. To eventually support my passion for gene therapy studies on human aging and I want to build my business to a global level and collaborate with like-minded individuals to support my project. I see this as a breakthrough project that could one day be a great achievement for humanity.

It is clear that I have a strong entrepreneurial spirit and a deep interest in science and innovation. By pursuing my own business, I have the opportunity to take ownership of my ideas and bring them to life on my own terms. I admire myself that I am using my skills and resources to pursue a project that I believe could make a positive impact on society.

If I am able to successfully collaborate with other like-minded individuals, I may be able to bring my project to a wider audience and attract the resources and support needed to take it to the next level. It will likely require a lot of hard work and dedication, but I am up for the challenge.

Always remember: Many will discourage you, but you have to be strong enough to move on. Try to do your best to cope with your passion and convert it into a tangible achievement. No matter who says what, trust yourself and discuss your plans only with those who can contribute and support you with proper advice. Surround your environment with positivity, have a clear mind, and avoid negative vibes, as that will deviate you from your chosen direction. You do not need to prove anything to anyone except yourself, and if you manage to do that, it is enough!

Chapter 18
Being Positive!

Sometimes, certain bad circumstances turn into something incredibly good, a blessing in disguise. At times, life brings us to a point where we feel displeasure, anger, annoyance, disturbed, and helpless. Have you ever gone out of your way to help someone, and it backfired to eventually land you in a better place? It's a strong belief if one's intention is right, no matter how hostile and unethical the situation gets, it still tends to be in one's favour. A positive person knows that everything that happens for the best, and I have experienced it.

After the initial commencement of INAS EXIM in UAE, I traveled home to Ukraine for my summer holidays. The warm ambiance of family and friends, glasses of red in the evenings, and traditional food… It was and always has been the best moment of my holidays planned once a year, catching up with relatives and friends, how life is… Time is always great during vacations! This also helps to keep my origin roots revitalized, helping my children to understand the culture and traditions that we have grown up with. It's a special time of the year for me.

One fine relaxing afternoon, I got a message on my phone that was shocking. The message was from my bank that one of my issued cheques was dishonored due to a lack of funds in my account. I could not understand how and what had happened; who did I issue the cheque to? Trying to recollect the given amount matched to the cheque issued to my client from Jordan as a guarantee cheque for his shipment. But that was done, and his payments had already been made had my doubts as I had worked with him for a few years and had also helped him during challenges—It couldn't be him! He had no reason to deposit the cheque? I had planned to collect the cheque once I was back from my holidays as I knew the client and trusted the owner. What troubled me was that the amount matched the guarantee cheque that I had issued to him, and I couldn't think of anyone else. So I called the owner of the company to enquire.

He seemed to be very naïve and in a state of denial, stating the cheque was with his finance manager, and he did not think it had been deposited…but the way he spoke made me doubt him. The cheque was handed to him based on total trust, and to say it was with his finance manager seemed okay, but why would it be deposited? Well, I was miles away and didn't have much choice but to wait to go back and check what the issue was. All I did for my balance vacation was to plan to go back to understand what had happened. My vacation had already been ruined by just wanting to go back so restlessly. Tensed by the whole issue, I needed to dig up what had gone wrong!

To give some background on this cheque, this was against a shipment of my regular client in Jordan. My company was shipping them goods regularly, but due to a change in some municipal regulations that were applied with immediate effect, the last shipment got rejected by the customs in Jordan, and they were asked to return the cargo or re-export it to another destination. The products were in absolutely perfect condition, but the labels were not as per the new regulations, hence, the rejection. The goods were paid for in advance, and the client had three options: one, to destroy the consignment completely, the easiest way out and that would be 100% loss on the shipment; two: to re-ship the shipment back to the country of origin (to the manufacturer) which was very complicated as the factory that exported them didn't have import permissions, and the third was to re-export the goods to any other country. But for that, we needed to find a potential buyer who was willing to take the full shipment, preferably in the MENA region. The only feasible solution that could be implied was to find a potential buyer in the region to help save total loss on the shipment.

My client panicked. Even though they had offices in other GCC countries, including Dubai in the United Arab Emirates, my suggestion to them was to ship it to other GCC branches. They didn't have the confidence to organize the shipment to be re-exported. So I jumped to their rescue, even though it was not something that concerned me since we had shipped the goods as per the instructions of the client. Yet, I wanted to help. Many say it is my weakness, but I feel it has always been my strength to get involved with any issues, even after the sale/deal is completed, especially if it pertains to a shipment/s from INAS. In this way, I ensure the comfort of my clients and go out of my way to support them in the best possible manner. This is how INAS has built its reputation among its clients.

Not knowing what exactly I could do with the shipment, I still took the commitment to help them. To my surprise, instead of appreciating my efforts, from the next day, the client started to pressurize me as if it was my obligation, stating that they had been doing business with us and we needed to help them out, and if we didn't, they would close all relationships with our establishment. Under the circumstances, I gave the owner some leverage, understanding his panic and pressure by tolerating his very haughty attitude. My mind was genuinely set on helping him out; my plan was on selling the goods to another client from the neighbouring countries and solving the issue as that seemed to be the best solution for it. But in reality, I had no clue on such short notice whom I should approach that could help me.

I had someone in mind who may have the capacity and the capabilities to support me in this situation. Not that we had established any past business together, but somehow, he had something that gave me the confidence that he may help with the present situation. He was none other than Vinay Gandhi—the owner of Golden Star International. I went to him as one business owner to another to explain the situation. I felt in my bones that he was prepared to negotiate with me knowing the situation, especially when it came to the price and payment terms. But somewhere, I knew that if I could make him agree, he had the potential to support me in the current situation. It was not hard to reconnect with him, as he has always been an easy person to approach for business. So I met him and offered him a trade deal, proposing that if he supported me, I should give him the distribution in the region of UAE for the brand.

In the past, we have had ample discussions for various projects, which rarely saw the daylight. Being a traditional businessman, he was a hard negotiator. I had stopped believing that I could ever sell anything to him. But I took this as an opportunity to see if we could work together and perhaps use the situation to open doors for possible business. Somewhere, deep down in my head, I was wondering whether my strategy to approach him as an entrepreneur would be more effective. Perhaps, being a business owner, he would understand the challenge of another business owner.

When I met him and explained the situation, to my surprise, he was not bargaining but was genuinely concerned about things. He was also trying to understand and help, and his major concerns suddenly seemed very valid. As any businessman would think, he was trying to protect his interest; his fears were of blocking funds, blocking storage, and payments, as this line of product was not his mainstream product line. What I liked about him at that moment was that he was being reasonable and he was explaining his challenges and concerns, which were true, and I voluntarily opted to support him, providing him the leverage to pay for the shipment after it was sold. It was a realistic approach, I felt. He wanted to honestly help me out. I committed that if he takes the goods, I shall reciprocate by helping him with the sales too. He knew I would, judging the way I was trying to help the Jordan client. I was happy he trusted me with my commitments. It felt like the business understanding was very mutual, and with that, to my surprise, he agreed to import the product.

I was flabbergasted! Never expected that. First, the shipment issue was sorted, and over that, it was sold to someone with whom I had never thought I would get a break to start a business. I have to admit, under all situations and discussions; I never found him to be hesitant or doubtful to forward selling the shipment. He just wanted to protect his business interest, regardless. He was taking the risk of blocking his storage space, and he was giving his commitment that he was not certain how much time it would take to sell the complete consignment. Even though he was not paying for the goods, he would still pay the clearing charges from the port, and storage charges of the shipment, putting time, effort, and logistics behind something he had never sold. On my part, I was taking the risk of giving him the leverage to pay later. What if he was not able to sell? Even though that was not something I believed, people tend to take things easy on products that they didn't pay for, so both of us had taken our share of risk on the other, based just on words of assurance and trust. Voilà! The shipment was sent to his company in the UAE from Jordan.

Meantime, my Jordanian client kept pestering me on guarantees and securities on the payment for the shipment even though it was not my obligation. It was becoming a nightmare; I was just genuinely trying to find a solution for him, but the pressure was tremendous, and he convinced me to issue a guarantee cheque for the value of the consignment, assuring he would keep it safe with him. I was confident that we would be able to sell the shipment in the United Arab Emirates, so, just to give him some kind of a guarantee, I issued him a undated cheque for the value of the shipment. Today, if you ask me why I did it, I have no clue. The Jordanian client had no choice; maybe he would have destroyed the shipment. Anyway, the two reasons why I agreed to give him the cheque were: *one*, he made me feel obligated, and *second*, as I mentioned, I was confident that Golden Star International could sell the goods. In any case, I had managed to hit two birds with one stone. I helped out my Jordanian client, and finally, I got a breakthrough to work with Golden Star International.

The shipment finally reached and was cleared by the experienced logistic team of Golden Star without any issues. To my surprise and delight, it was a tremendous joint effort, and we managed to sell the goods quicker than I had ever imagined and that too, at a decent margin. This order even helped me bag a new repeat order from them. I had my foot grounded in Golden Star International. INAS had a new client, the first in the region of the United Arab Emirates.

Coming back to the cheque, once I reached back to UAE, I immediately investigated about the bounced cheque and to my surprise, I came to know that Golden Star had an old issue with my Jordanian client's UAE office. They had bought some goods and had quality issues that had led to a dispute between them, and they were in constant debates over discounts and compensation as Golden Star had exported the goods. My client taking advantage of having my guarantee cheque used me as a medium to get his outstanding dues by depositing my cheque and getting it dishonoured from the bank to use it as a legal threat. It was a very unprofessional way to do things, and the past dispute had nothing to do with me or my company INAS.

Perhaps he did not imagine that Golden Star would so efficiently clear the shipment and sell it, too, even though I had proposed the same to him in the beginning, asking him to re-ship the goods to his UAE office. At that time, he was not confident. Maybe, he regretted that he had missed the opportunity and lost the chance of distribution in the UAE, or he just very conveniently used my cheque against an old dispute with Golden Star, forgetting how I supported and helped him out during his emergency.

What had happened in the past between his company and Golden Star didn't concern me or my company in any way. Why involve me into it? I had not informed Golden Star about my guarantee cheque earlier as it was something between my Jordanian client and me, and as far as they were concerned, the full payments of this consignment were successfully done to the Jordanian client, and the past issues still needed to be dealt with between them without any concern to me. After the money was received for the consignment professionally, ethically and morally and in good faith, he should have returned my cheque back to me.

When I shared this concern with Golden Star, they were quick to resolve the matter, and even though they knew they had been treated unfairly by my Jordanian client's UAE office, they paid the company its dues just to help me get my cheque back from them.

This experience was an eye-opener that made me understand that it is very rare to find people who can be trusted in the business world. I have never done business with that Jordanian client due to his unfair approach towards the situation. Also, he has not been in touch with me after this incident due to the way he had misused my trust. It is surprising to see how people are ready to behave so immorally for short-term gains. Perhaps, they do so to prove to themselves how smart they are in business, losing all ethics and values.

On the one hand, this incident helped me understand that I need not go overboard to help someone based purely on good faith, and on the other, it taught me that if someone is doing something with good intentions, the results always turn out in their favour. My positive approach and the right intentions not only helped me gain a new customer but also a genuine friend who helped me throughout the ordeal, with honest efforts.

"Stay positive and keep your intentions right. No matter how things look, it shall eventually turn out to be in your best favour."

Chapter 19
How to Create a Highly Successful Start-Up

Success is what the majority of people would like to achieve in diverse matters. But what do you need to be a successful entrepreneur, and how do you gain a specific set of skills to be one? This is an important subject to think about before you start any kind of business venture.

Know yourself and self-analyze to know if you are capable and if you have it within you. This is because your business is a long-term project that requires dedication and commitment—perhaps even a stronger commitment than marriage, a commitment equal to parental responsibility. This is why the term/phrase in the business world when addressing a project is: "It's my baby!" The kind of care, patience, love, and responsibility you will need will be equal, if not greater, than what is needed when parenting a child.

One needs to be passionate. Passion is the best fuel for starting your business. It kicks you to work towards your dreams. Persistence will bring in discipline, but passion is not only about your routine work; it is something that shall give you the drive. Disregard if your passion seems unachievable at some stage of life, but make it the fuel for what you want to achieve. Don't forget to look back, at times, to see how far you have come, but never get disappointed if your progress has been slow. Slow progress is far better than no progress at all. Keep your aims higher, and do not underestimate yourself.

Time management, responsibility, and organized planning: I guess being from the Soviet Union culture, everything is enrooted in my systems; plans, and schedules. But this has to be embedded in you right from the start, and I have seen most business owners are well organized in their own customized manner. It does not need to be something that is only there because it is cultivated within you right from childhood, nor is it that if people have it within them, they will be great business achievers. Nevertheless, this is an important aspect and a plus point when you start all on your own.

I have seen traditional business people writing appointments on a desk planner and successful businessmen hiring secretaries to keep notes on everything that needs to be done. The advantage is: if you are organized, you have time to focus on other, more important things, and it gives you more time to pay attention to major things that will help develop your business more than just daily sequences.

My modern business life is well organized. I cannot imagine a day without a calendar on my laptop. All meetings have reminders, and I plan my calendar considering timings for lunch breaks, road trips, and even waiting times. Also, keeping an A4 paper with a list of notes for important things to keep track of during the day, has become a daily routine. Before closing my laptop and leaving the office, I screen the list, erase-accomplished tasks, and transfer the rest to the next day's to-do list.

<u>Vision</u>: The very beginning of any great idea always starts with a <u>vision</u>. Vision is the simple answer to the question of why! Why am I doing it, and what is my goal? Believe in your vision and work towards it, for if you don't, no one else will. My vision was to get an overseas job, and I chose the path of learning English to use it as a medium to help reach my vision. I started to study English as a second language. I believed it was the gateway to travel the world. Life is full of diverse possibilities. At that point in life, all I wanted was to use the English language to support me and get an international job. My focus and belief in it were undivided and total. It took time, patience, and persistence, but it never crossed my mind to ever give up until I had reached my goal.

It was a long shot, but, in the end, I made it, and English was among the most important media that helped me to get my very first break in an export organization, which eventually helped to pave my way to my first successful overseas job. I worked hard to fulfill it, and I accomplished all tasks towards my vision. Maybe, it was not as fast or easy as I would have liked it to be, but it also helped me exercise my persistence, dedication, and determination.

Once we have managed to reach our targets, we should enhance our vision. Remember, after a meal, the mighty crocodile feels sluggish as if it is drugged, and anyone can go close to it, even touch it, take advantage of it, and even hunt it. Don't get sluggish and allow your appetite to die, feeling satisfied. You can rest but cannot stop. Keep creating new tasks; give yourself new targets that need to be achieved. The most classic example that comes to my mind is that of the leader of Dubai, H. H. Sk. Mohammed Bin Rashid Al Maktoum, who makes me proud to be a part of this ever-growing nation. With his vision, he has kept initiating new targets for Dubai. No matter how many targets Dubai has accomplished, you will find new ones to look forward to, a true example of a business leader.

My visions are variable all the time. Some of them are achieved and parked, while some are getting added as new challenges; life is constantly in momentum. Vision gives you direction, and you must build the steps towards it, keeping yourself focused and firm, expecting results, and believing in them. While you are starting any kind of business setup, you should think about the purpose of creating your company, what your short-term and long-term goals are, and how you plan to fulfill your dreams. This has been the mantra that I follow, and this mantra has taken me from a small town in Ukraine to where I am today.

<u>Being creative:</u> Having just a vision is a start, but not sufficient to succeed. Anyone can dream and imagine, but one has to work towards it and being <u>creative</u> is among the keys to success. Be creative, think different from the crowd with new ideas, finding solutions to obstacles, and differentiating yourself from others.

Creativity generates new ideas, and these ideas should be practical and implemented into reality. This is the way one can accelerate towards the success of a business. It is important to keep your mind open to new ideas and discuss them with like-minded friends, relatives, and associates. At times, it would sound silly at first, but it does not mean it can't happen. Keep a broad vision; express it and think over it. I remember discussing my idea of a dress made of recyclable material with my business partner for a talent competition during my pageant show. It all sounded a little silly at first, but moving forward, he guided me with materials that could be used and helped me enhance my vision towards it. It is among my best and proudest achievements. Later, the same idea helped me develop and create a company that makes environmentally and ocean-friendly wall mounts under the brand name '*Mystique*'. No idea, big or small, can or should be underestimated. But one has to be <u>patient.</u> Not everyone can always see from your point of view, especially if your ideas are fresh and original.

<u>Patience:</u> We have all been taught patience is a virtue. But patience is also valuable. I believe being a woman, the greatest gift I got was to be trained in patience, an experience gained while having my first child. For sure, knowing my nature, I kept reading a lot of materials and tried to prepare myself for parenthood, but one can never prepare enough. With all the readings I did, I had never handled an infant. You cannot learn bicycle by reading a book.

The experience of understanding an infant was a blessing. Right from seeing him taking his first breath into this wonderful world to embracing his new environment, everything was different: The way he sensed me, the sense of smell, touch, voice, and how he reacted, was an experience far from describing. All so amazing!

Just for a few days until reality kicks in, and believe me, it kicks in pretty fast! Sleepless nights, changing him in the middle of the night, trying to understand him, burping him after a feed…it came to a point I am not shy to admit that I started to doubt if this was my child or they had changed him in the hospital!

His experience ended up teaching me Patience and Tolerance. I realize that without it, I could have never developed the values so strongly. Putting the same to practice in business today when I don't see results, as at times things get very frustrating, I remind myself of the times that I had gone through, and everything else looks so minuscule in comparison to it.

You have to give time for results – Good things take time!

Plan and strategize:

Using every opportunity that life gave me, I helped develop myself. Another great example that my motherhood taught me was to strategize. When I cannot manage a situation, I try to be calm. During early motherhood, with all the office pressure, I was at the peak of going into desperation. It was then that I started thinking about how to reduce my pressure and what had to be done. I started to develop a strategy. Office pressure, I realized, was something that was not totally in my hands, but at home, to handle my newborn, I started monitoring his sleep patterns, adjusting my routine towards it, and having the chance to have sufficient time to restore my energy. This helped me a lot in becoming strong. What I learned is that in any situation, you have to be patient enough to keep your mind at peace. Monitor, analyze, don't overreact, be observant, and you will find a solution.

When you are in business, you must learn to manage people and make them perform, despite challenges. They are the media through which you get to the final goal. That's how you develop your strategy, and that should always be your focus to help you accomplish your goals.

What and how to talk to people and keeping in mind their mindset, you must make sure they will receive information the way you want them to by being a good communicator both to your clients and your team alike. It is an important factor, and good communication is only possible if you have the patience to understand and plan to customize your strategies for every individual.

<u>Being Persuasive:</u> It is an important part of a successful business. And you can't be persuasive unless you believe in it yourself first. To believe in it, you should be convinced by it. After achieving success, you start believing more in yourself. The more steps of success you climb, the more confident you feel.

When I was sure about my products after successfully selling them in Jordan and Oman, I could convince my partner in UAE to take the full shipment from Jordan. He, as a businessman with years of experience behind him, must have been influenced by my persuasive approach. Maybe there were other factors to it, but my persuasiveness played a major role in the negotiations.

Now I can firmly say that I have a strong ability to convince people because of the experiences that I have obtained while creating my start-up from scratch. This has and shall keep helping me develop and initiate new ideas, find better ways and means, and help grow my company.

Self-motivation While you believe in yourself, it is also important for you to keep motivating yourself by pushing and promoting yourself…reminding yourself what you are, where you are, why you started, and where you want to be in life. Achieving goals should not be your only target, but setting new goals and improving should be a continuous effort. This can only be possible if one keeps motivating one's own self. Be focused with all your energy. In case things are not going your way, stop, recharge, rest, but never quit. Like everyone, I have days when things seem to be falling apart. That is the time I remind myself where I am, how I reached here, and the challenges I faced.

I remember when I was a new nursing mother, and I had to give my exams in Ukraine, where I needed to travel over six hours by train and change buses; my family and friends objected to my travel, but I motivated myself, reminding myself how important it was for me to do it; how I had put my hard work and efforts to prepare for the exams. I took it upon myself to travel the distance, gave my genetic engineering exams and on the same day, came back to my state. It took willpower and self-motivation, constantly reminding myself to be focused on completing my exams. That qualification later helped me to relate the characteristics of cows milk. That again helped me engineer and develop a new modified recipe for commercial cheeses, which we successfully distribute in the region of MENA now.

Life is full of obstacles, but just remember that you are bigger than that!

It has indeed never been a joy ride to set up the business, especially when one experiences the kind of challenges that I had gone through. Given that I have mothered my two wonderful gifts during the journey, that was not at all easy. Yes, emotions play a vital role in your success and failures, but you have to learn to grow above your emotions. Easier said than done! Our focus should be bigger than our emotions, bigger than our egos, and bigger than the urge to just do or copy others. The determination, the passion, and above all, the thrill and kick you get out of achievement is what should make the difference for you.

The fun of being the founder is always that you are responsible. You are the captain of the ship, and you need to reach a point. You can find fruits at the end of the journey or cactus. So, my advice is: you better learn to make Cactus Salad; you never know when you will need the skill!

As I noticed, women in business have a unique skill set since they are naturally born to survive and nurture future generations to continue the life circle. Only because of their natural instincts their business mindset is largely oriented towards social contribution. Women create business groups, support each other, and promote social startups, workshops, webinars, clubs around the world, and PR and marketing companies. Even the United Nations has an UN-WOMEN platform as a base to empower women for greater achievements and many more. Taking the opportunities and the advantages of this privilege, a woman today can help herself reach new heights of achievement, touching the peak of success.

Chapter 20
Out of Sight, Out of Mind! Visibility Matters

Launching your company is just the first chapter. As you progress, you have to be visible in your network and grow the network. This is an important strategy and will help you expand your wings and you to the next level.

INAS—International Network for Achievable Solution—a creation of my own from scratch! I have constantly been thinking about how to develop my connections through references, searching for new leads to convert opportunities into potential clients to help build the network and grow along. All the business was built purely based on networking, meeting people, and references, but it had its limitations. However, I realized that the global potential of networking is beyond a region and the limitations of a geographical area. So, it needed more networking with people and my ability to understand the demand for my products in various markets, utilizing my experience, knowledge, and skills. But, there was something that was missing, something that was so important and I could never get my finger on.!!

As a woman, building a network was never a challenge, but building the right network is what makes all the difference. A lot of time is wasted on inquiries and requirements from people bragging about how they can help, how they can connect me to other buyers, and a lot of other mumbo jumbos. Filtering real potential clients, and serious business people, is always a dare, and this requires a skill set that one learns over time.

During the COVID-19 Pandemic, when almost the whole globe was shut for a few months, I was trying to make the best use of the time, trying to build my network and at times getting frustrated with filtering true potential clients. My business ally, a good friend, and a reliable business partner were aware of my efforts. One day, out of the blue, I received a message from him. It was a registration link to a website with the application form to participate in a women empowerment contest. Since the time we started to work closely, he has always been supportive and helped lift me during challenges, guiding me and giving helpful suggestions, ideas and advice, but what was this? Pushing me to participate in a pageant contest? I have never felt it was for me. I didn't take it seriously.

As a teenager, I had some experience back home in Ukraine of being on a catwalk and acting as a photo model (non-commercial) for a local beauty pageant. All that was just the whims and fancies of a young teenager and didn't last long. It was never something in terms of a career or profession or a subject I had ever spoken about with him. It was just a faded part of my teenage memories. I was still looking at the message and could not understand why my business partner had sent this to me.

I thought that, at this point, it was just a joke, but he called me to elaborate on his idea. Suggesting the link was towards a platform that initiates women will help to give me the confidence to become a powerful spokesperson. The contest was all about empowerment rather than just another banal beauty pageant. Participation was not considered by age or marital status; it was all about equality and self-knowledge to discover yourself and your real potential. He was confident this would help boost my self-image. He told me, "What do you have to lose? You know yourself, and it's an opportunity." He also added he believed in me and that this would help open new doors both for INAS EXIM and as an individual for myself.

He was right. I had nothing to lose; if I was not comfortable at the start, I would just quit. He successfully convinced me by explaining to me the advantages of my exposure to the event. My thoughts went even beyond what he was trying to elaborate on. Maybe it was an opportunity for me to link my causes and do something for society, to highlight global challenges along with it, an opportunity to bring visibility of my company internationally. As he kept explaining, I got more ideas and started to see his point of view and the potential that this platform could help me achieve. I filled out the application form and sent a confirmation to participate. It did not take time for me to be called for my first online interview. In the interview, it felt I really needed to discover myself and wanted to see how much potential I had within me to take this opportunity and help achieve my visibility to the world. It was something that challenged me, and I got thrilled about the participation already.

What else can I wish for? I had an experienced business partner whom I respected, and he seemed to have full confidence in me. I already had a fan, to begin with; all I needed was a few thousand more (haha!). But at that stage, I needed to do something important in my life, and participating in this contest could provide me with the challenge and the drive that I felt was suddenly missing during the lockdown. A great platform, something that could break the ice and take me and my company to the next level. I was accepted as a participant and qualified in all the requirements necessary, and it all happened so fast that before I knew it, I was already in it, looking forward to being in the Grand Finale.

It was easy to be selected and short-listed, as all my qualifications met the selection criteria. Being an entrepreneur, having my own company, academic qualifications, and other such standards that benchmarked the initial qualifying criteria helped me accelerate towards the final round faster, but the challenge had just begun. A lot of it was manageable, and most required skill sets like public speaking and wearing your confidence were a sure short thing. The most challenging part during the competition was to take a call and prepare a 1-2 minute performance scene at the time of a talent show, and the given preparation period was really short.

I could not cope with an idea of what to present and how to present it. My mind was stuck, limited towards dancing, singing, and as such, performing on the stage. This was never my cup of tea. Something unique was required, something I stood for, something with a message, but nothing was coming to my head. The time was drawing closer and closer towards the final date.

I started to think about my purpose of doing something for society, and it struck me that the biggest challenge in the World is climate change. We know every religion in the world teaches us to love and respect Nature, not to take more than required from it, preserve it, value it… Our ancestors seemed to be more advanced and knowledgeable with their noble thoughts! Today it looks like we have forgotten those values. We can't differentiate our wants from our needs and keep exploiting nature beyond our requirements.

So, I planned to utilize the platform and decided to speak about the challenges our planet faces and to use this opportunity to send a message to the world to accept nature, not abuse it! That was the key to generating an idea and getting ready for the talent show! **With a few respectful**

<u>**changes, we can make a huge impact in the world we live in today, the world we will leave for our children.**</u> To show my contribution towards my stand at the event, I planned to wear a dress made with recycled paper and jute thread. This idea was inspired by watching paper recyclers collecting empty boxes from our warehouse. The idea stuck with me; I could use these boxes to make myself a dress.

I started working on designs, drawing patterns, and taking different materials to see what could be used. As a girl, I was always creative and such challenges were a thrill. Initially, I tried a few things, such as using glue, normal thread, and paper tape to see how I could fix the dress…but that didn't help. I needed something that would be strong enough to hold and at the same time give a bit of flexibility; it should be a natural material. Finally, I thought a jute thread would do the trick! Taking over 40 hard-working hours from a busy career mom's life, I finally finished the dress…with a purpose to deliver a message to the World!

It will make me happy if my efforts would make a small impact on my message to the World… Let us all stand for a greener, safer and respect for our planet. To help spread the message, I thought of making a short video **https://www.youtube.com/watch?v=oW4ncImlAe0** to share with the world. The video shows the stages and techniques of how I managed to make the dress.

At first, I had no clue how to make, alter, or edit videos; it took a lot of learning to combine material and make trailers out of pieces of information to create something holistic. This was also one of many skill sets that I learned for participating in the contest. The event helped me understand better the power of social media platforms and how to create short stories, videos, presentations, etc., to express my business goals for the targeted audience. I started to change my way of handling business and re-innovate personal social media platforms to more business-oriented media.

It was the grand finale, and I already had changed a lot of my perception of the world, the media, and my approach. I had already gained much from the experience, and whether I got an award or title was suddenly not of much significance. However, the icing on the cake was that I obtained the title of **'The Best Personality'** and was awarded **Second Runners-up** for the contest. With the win, I got great exposure in the media. This also helped me be more confident with my own social media connections, and I also started promoting my company. My mind started to think globally, deviate my strategies, change my perception from a red ocean to a blue ocean approach, and understand the requirements of new potential markets thanks to international visibility.

Never underestimate yourself. Always give yourself a challenge that you think is not easy to achieve, and a good friend is always someone who lifts you. As Oprah Winfrey quoted, "Surround yourself only with people who are going to lift you higher."

Once I got the hang of it, I started to use my skills to connect with other media. Soon I got connected with some very powerful international platforms, which helped me connect further, helping me to form a stronger and wider network. Connecting with like-minded individuals to support the growth of both my business and my influence through the channels also got me opportunities to meet some heroic figures behind the networks. I did online courses on social media and participated in other global challenges and campaigns. I started to see mild results, reflecting on my business. My existing customers started to follow my news on social media channels, encouraging new developments which my company was working on. We started to advertise online on different platforms. I started to get new requirements for new lines of products. Proudly, INAS launched organic feed as a line of a sustainable living concept further developed a brand, 'Mystique'—an elegant wall decoration made from 100% Natural, Re-cycled, Bio-degradable, Ocean Friendly material; and we have so many new ideas and concepts yet to be disclosed and many still to be discovered.

All this taught me a great deal and gave me an idea of what is required to gain credibility in one's niche to be a successful entrepreneur. One needs to have a vision for long-term goals. And now, it was time for me to share my thoughts and ideas with people who feel stagnated and with those who don't feel the confidence to start on their own. Hence, I thought the best way was to write a book and share my escapades of business life co-authoring with someone with a richer experience and exposure, a friend and also a business ally—Vinay Gandhi.

A book was of our journey through all our challenges of start-up establishment, ups and downs that led us to work as partners. Now the challenge was bigger… My business ally pushed me to participate in a Women's Empowerment Pageant, and after the successful experience, reciprocatively, I pushed him to jointly write a business book with me. It was not as simple as it sounds. I was like a matador taking the bull by the horns! Convincing him and his strong-headed (bull-headed) personality was tough. By the way, his 'Never say die!' attitude has made him a lot what he is today.

But, I also knew he has the skillset for authoring a book, the rich experience, and his exposure could help a lot of people to learn and understand many things about business. Persuading him that the whole groundwork of publishing shall be managed by me, taking the responsibility of marketing, I convinced him that all he had to do was write, explaining to him the advantages of writing a business book and how it might help his business. That was the only thing I could think of, to break through to him.

The best part what I like about our collaboration is once we agree, we work for it as a team; we work together as one. It's never about pointing fingers or egos. If it is successful, it is a joint effort, and if it is not, it's a joint learning. We take equal responsibility, and even though I committed to marketing the book, he has always been with me, suggesting, guiding, and discussing things. Our strength of synchronizing our actions has become our most powerful asset. We think about mutual success, irrespective of whose idea it was or who takes the merit for it. We both are not into taking small credits. Our focus is always on the eventual result of success. Filling each other's gaps to bring the best out of each other and eventually bringing the best possible results to our ventures is the aim.

In this case, one has a wider raw material of thoughts with a richer experience, and the other has a wider network with an option to reach further. He always knew that visibility is important but thought it could be purchased, which is true to a great extent. Being in business for 20+ years, he has built up his work purely on references and relationships. Now he sees a new angle to it, and he trusts me and values my opinion, so he opted to go along with it. Plus, he is not afraid to try new territories for business development and being along with a known devil like me. He has done it before and has achieved great success with it. Need the success of our first shipment be reminded?!😝☺

Chapter 21
The Mantra of a Business Partnership

In most cases, a business partner would be a friend, a colleague, a family, or a business ally. Whomever the person would be, once you have decided to incorporate a partnership with them, you should be prepared with certain guidelines. It has never been an easy task to merge two mindsets and manage individualism. Every person has a specific background and expertise that should be considered and respected, focusing on strengths and weaknesses to help go in the right direction to achieve harmony and satisfaction in the business set-up. So, what do you need to know, and how should one reciprocate to feel a comfort level in leading a successful project jointly?

To follow my observations, partners should be thinking differently, yet the goal should be common. If I am being aggressive—a 'go-getter' type on a project, my partner should be more analytical and observant. Simultaneously, if my partner is more bullish on a project, I feel I should take the seat of the observant. This is a hard-to-find combination and also, in many ways, foolproof, as the points of view are different and then combined to a common holistic view. Everything should be balanced as day and night, black and white, hot and cold, man and woman, aggressive and obliging, yin and yang. It is important to achieve a successful equilibrium in business.

Be focused on your common goal: Partners have started a business to generate profit, and this is the ultimate final result of all dealings and actions. Utilize each other's knowledge and different ways of thinking. That is the biggest advantage. Yes, we have diversified approaches, but that is what makes us stronger and unique in finding the right solutions.

For instance, we had a supplier through whom we imported our first container of assorted food products in cash to UAE. After we successfully sold the goods, we decided that we could work further to expand market distribution, but on credit terms, as UAE is predominantly a credit market. Despite numerous negotiations, meetings, and overseas trips for discussions, nothing was going in the right direction. Our supplier was hesitant to agree on certain payment terms, kept negotiating, and kept changing his mind, and the final decision to sign a contract and ship goods on credit seemed far beyond achievement.

Finally, it reached a point where my partner gave up on it, but I was persistent and believed that all the efforts we had put into the project couldn't go to waste. I felt the weakness of the supplier was trust. They were willing to work with us, but for some reason, they were half-hearted in taking their final decision. I was not able to figure out what was going on and how to fix it, but I was not going to give up on it so easily. So, I started to interact by myself, and my partner did not mind. He always had a very sarcastic look and would just smile when I would update him on any discussion between the supplier and me. He never discouraged me and did not intervene. He had trust in me but was not very optimistic about the supplier. He understood me and called me a tough nut for the project. What I liked about him is he didn't interfere or discourage me. He used to hear me out, and, in the end, he would say: "You have the patience, and I have run out of it, so I respect you handling it."

I kept my relationship going and even purchased a few consolidated shipments on cash from the supplier to keep the flame burning. It took me nearly eighteen months to finally crack the company down through my communication, and the day finally came when we got confirmation on payment terms, and eventually, we signed a contract with the company. It took a lot of effort, determination, hard work, and strategy for me to finally melt them down, but it was worth the effort as I got a positive result from it. The moment the contract was signed, both of us were already discussing the next stage of how to unitize this opportunity to help business growth, how to promote the brand, and where to promote the brand.

My partner congratulated me on my accomplishment, but we never stopped to discuss whose achievement it was or who gets the credit for it. All of this becomes irrelevant; our focus remains on the common goal, and we do not wait to get recognized for every single individual achievement, no matter how big or small it may be. We have a common goal set in our minds, and that is what it is!

Know when to give space and learn to trust: It is required to give space to your partner and trust their instinct. In our case, my partner felt that I believed in it. Even though he was skeptical, he did not discourage me; he allowed me to go with my gut feeling and felt that I could manage the situation, thus leaving things in my hands. It is not that he got frustrated or wanted to prove any point to show that he knew better. He just allowed the project to be in my hands. He also explained to me that if it did not work out, we would waste our joint efforts, and if it had to work, it would work even by one of our efforts, and the better choice to pursue it was me, as I was completely into it and felt being more competent to excel in it.

Sometimes, people need time to understand the situation, adjust strategies, and develop techniques.

Additional opinions may block the thinking process or influence other party decisions, and the results may not be that effective. As they say, "Too many cooks spoil the broth!" So, it is also important for you or your partner to know when to step back in a situation and who should get to lead on a project while having total faith in the other.

Know Strengths: One has to understand that you are working with your partner because they have a certain strength that is better than the other. It is best to delegate roles to get the best possible results. My partner and I have differences without which we will not be able to fill gaps for each other, and we recognize and acknowledge that.

In one case, we had a prospective lead for organic animal feed requirements for a local farm. We found a reliable source from the USA and offered the product to the farm. Knowing my strength, I knew I could study business cases, analyze, and do market strategies, but things like negotiations are not of my preference or liking. I do not have the patience and the nerve for it. Without a second thought, I involved my partner in discussions. He enjoys negotiation and takes it as a challenge, understanding the psychology of the client, their break-points, and their capacities. He could debate based on quality, volumes, schemes, packaging…the list is endless. His way of handling a negotiation is so diverse, pitching in from every angle. After handing over the client to him, I took a step back and allowed him to do all the dialogues. We were discussing the cost jointly, and at a stage, we had to give a presentation to the client at his office, which I prepared for him, but he remained the front face knowing what to offer and how much to discount it. It took him a fair amount of time to close the first deal, but he finally closed the transaction on a good note. Today, this has become one of our highlighted product lines in and around the region, and we are growing in the category by giant strides, partnering with one of the largest organic animal feed producers in the United States. All this was only possible because we knew each other's strengths, and that helped fill the gaps, as also remaining working strongly focused on the results to achieve a common target.

No space for the ego: The strongest requirement when working with a partner is that all should be so strongly interlocked and work as one so that there is no space for egos. This is the best manner to handle a partnership. There is nothing to be ashamed of or act superior about. I can happily hand over work to my partner if I feel he can do it better than I can, and I happily accept in return something he feels I can do better. We can sit and discuss our strengths and our weaknesses and not get offended. Yes, at times, we do have disagreements and debates, and in some very rare cases, disputes and arguments, but it is just a part of the job. At the end of it all, no matter what, it always ends up as a healthy understanding where we mutually recognize that the communication done is not to show anyone down but to help lift the shortcoming of the other and improve for the better.

The reciprocation towards each other is only possible if both are on the same page keeping aside self-pride and at the same time supporting each other's self-esteem. If this is one-sided, then you will soon find a war of egos, with each trying to uphold, compete, and prove their points. If one does not manage and utilize the other partners' strengths and understand them as their own strengths, what is the point of having a business partner?

Do not compete: They say healthy competition is the best way to improve oneself, but your business partner and you are not competing, as you work as one mechanism. One can't drive a car if the carburetor is not aligned with the engine; if you are competing with your business partner, it can damage the results. I have learned with experience and have also seen a lot of companies where one partner thinks he knows better and refuses to take advice from another partner just because his or her experience is more.

Always hear out your partner, even though he or she may be less experienced or may not be as expert or skillful as you. Who knows, they may give you a whole new point of view to look from. Sometimes, we are so deep into an issue or situation or are so accustomed to handling something in a manner that we forget and overlook alternate possibilities. One has to learn to cooperate to help find solutions. Remember, you have a much higher aim to achieve than to compete with your business partner/s.

Accept criticism: No one is perfect and flawless. Always be open to learning, and to learn, one first also needs to be open to criticism. No matter how experienced you are, life provides us with a lesson that needs to be learned each day. This is where the business partnership between Vinay and me gels so well. I can share my opinions and know that they can be rejected or accepted...rejected for a valid reason, and at times he will accept it and try it out without feeling ashamed, or think why he didn't think of it, or stating he knows better, based purely on experience. If the plan or idea is good, it is implemented. In the same way, I feel blessed to be around someone whose opinion I can rely on and learn from.

Only people who wish for prosperity give advice and provide structural feedback. Such people provide healthy criticism to help improve you. What better than supporting, progressing, and growing with each other? In business, that is an important aspect of a healthy business partnership.

Being Honest and Being Fair: Honesty is the best policy! We have all heard this a million times, but how many people will tell you that Honesty and Fairness are two different aspects? A good business partner shall not only be honest but also fair. Being fair shows that you want your business partner to grow mutually. It is very easy to see partnerships where one partner struggles and the other does not bother to take the stress from him/her just because, as per the agreement, it is not under their portfolio or job profile to take on such responsibility. They do not understand that, at times, a small support and gesture can not only help boost and encourage the business partner but also create a strong unbreakable business block. It has happened many times in our partnership where we voluntarily suggest a fair transaction, understanding and keeping in mind the situation, nature, contribution, and many such contingencies.

Keep a positive attitude: This is applicable not only to business partnerships but also in general in everyday life. **Whatever may be the situation, just be positive** and make sure you choose a compatible business partner. **If we think we can, we are fifty percent there.** A positive attitude between partners helps support in every aspect. And no matter how positive you are, all days are not the same. We tend to face situations and have hurdles in our day-to-day business operations. During such times, there is nothing better than a partner who can pep you up during your gloomy days with the right attitude. Such business partners are a blessing.

During the COVID-19 Pandemic, while the whole world was in lockdown, we were facing tremendous losses. My partner was forced to close his restaurant division, and our food trading division was losing money. All staff was staying at home, and we were rotating staff and having work cycle weeks to help reduce our operation costs. During that period, our operations were kept to a bare minimum. Our Profit-and-Loss graph showed a depressing minus figure; we kept discussing possible ways to correct the situation. What I liked about that period was that we were staying sober, not panicking, and genuinely trying to see any way possible to survive the challenge. A lot of companies were cutting salaries and terminating employees. Our whole team felt depressed, yet understanding.

We started to look for different business opportunities, kept searching, connecting to a lot of digital platforms, and I found some online trading platforms and shared the idea of trading online with my partner. He was quick to grab the idea, and we saw a light of hope. Everyone started to get motivated. We developed new strategies to manage to keep the situation under check during the crisis. We, along with our team, put in a lot of effort and started seeing results. We started gaining new customers and new suppliers that helped us to sustain and face the prevailing challenges. It was the positive synergy that we shared which helped us not only to survive the challenge but also to grow when the whole world was complaining. We were committed to taking up the challenge and beating it too. Our positive attitude helped us surpass the phase with ease.

My synopsis of the right business partner: True business partners are like two children standing under a walnut tree. Both have a singular desire to get as many walnuts from the tree as possible. One is good at aiming and aiming at each walnut fruit, and the other takes a bunch of stones and throws them together, hoping to hit as many fruits as possible.

The walnut tree is the structure of the business. The two children under the tree are partners. The walnut is the fruit of business. Even though the skill sets and approaches are different, the target is the same. In the end, they collect the fruits and distribute them fairly. They do not discuss who managed to get what quantities of fruit. The focus is to work as a team and to collect the maximum walnuts from the tree and not on how one managed to get them. The trust between true partners is immense; they do not focus on the manner of how the other works but more on their belief in each other's way of working, and the focus is only on the end result.

This is how I felt about a true business partner. When I walked into Vinay's office after experiencing all the challenges I had faced, there was an energy that drew me to him. I had just a hunch that he would understand my position. To my amazement, he did and stood by during the time when it was required the most, and he did it intending to genuinely help me out. Over the period, we understood we were so different yet similar in many ways. Our business paths got us together again for a purpose, the purpose of helping build our empires together, without grudge or prejudice.

This is how I feel that the right synergies are formed to create an elite partnership!

Chapter 22
Resurgence of Rejuvenation

Nadiya Albishchenko, a very prominent and reputed name in the market, a lady I had met when she had just stepped into the industry, her first impression by far a lasting one. After a break, we reconnected to work on a few projects before she chose to take a leap and jump into starting on her own. She came to me when she was facing a challenge, seeking help with a shipment for one of her clients in Jordan. The funny thing is, while she was requesting and convincing me, she began to give all her support in terms of marketing and sales, basically to help someone else! She did remind me, in a lot of ways, of how I was when I started, and this attitude of mine had got me beaten to the ground many times.

But her sincerity and her sense of responsibility towards her customer were so genuine that I opted to support her as, somehow, I could relate to and understand her. I had only hoped she would not regret the efforts she was putting in to help her client, as I have burnt my hands doing so many times in the past. Unfortunately, my hunch came true, and her client eventually used her goodness to settle some old disputes with our company that were not even related to the shipment we had helped them with. This was a very unethical act and, in a way, beyond crossing the threshold of trust, especially with someone who went out of her way to support them during the time they needed it the most. It didn't come as a surprise for me, but I had genuinely wished I would be wrong about my intuition in this case. But as my mother often says, **<u>everything happens for a reason, and the reason is always good</u>**.

This experience made us work more closely with each other, and we started working as business allies on so many new projects. The trust between us as business partners grew stronger as the same was commonly based on the end results of our collaboration. Working with her has been an amazing experience. We synchronize well, supporting each other's shortcomings, and even though we have different ways of approaching our targets, our focuses are almost always the same. When I started associating with her, I came to know she is fair in her approach, something that is rare to find in people. The fact is, if you have an associate partner who is fair in approach and trusts you, it has to be reciprocated in the same manner to make the partnership work. Mostly, in my past business partnership experiences, I have learned it is usually that one of the partners tends to take advantage of the others and tries to over-smart them for short-term gains. With Nadiya, I found our points of view matched in so many ways that the best way to describe it is like comparing to a situation where we speak different languages yet pass on the same message.

Remember, partnership means mutual growth, something that most people easily forget, just to gain temporary benefits. The first shipment that we jumped into was purely to help and based only on an assurance from her. The commitment was honoured by her, giving her total support. It did not mean that we at Golden Star were just laid back and let her do the hard work and reap the benefits from it. We had put in equal efforts even though it was a shipment we had not invested in, but we cared and showed our genuineness by supporting it in every manner we could, thereby respecting the trust she had shown in us.

This was partnership at its best. The focus, the efforts, and the challenges were all discussed, with risks calculated and targets marked. This experience taught both of us a lot and helped us experience the essence of a true, reliable partnership. We started to get involved in new projects, working our way together and exploring new opportunities. Some met a silent death, some were a great success, yet what we enjoyed was working with each other, the endless discussions on improvements and developments, discussing facts, sharing experiences, understanding where we are, and setting targets to reach the next level, for with us only the sky is the limit. This has always been the mutual focal point of our progressive growth.

Nadiya and I both have some unique ideas of how and what we want from a project. A lot of times, we do not see eye to eye. Usually, when it comes to launching a new project, most of our projects do not start with a common view but, by far, with a common purpose in mind. All our projects go through mutual filtration, acceptance, approvals, discussion and then those exceptional ones that end up with just maybe, or perhaps later. Whatever it is, these deliberations are always respected, allowing space and time for each other's evaluation. Business is not only about numbers but also a lot about inner consciousness, and we understand that giving each other leverage over one's intuition is an integral part of a business partnership.

We have worked on some of the projects where she has been able to get breakthroughs with her consistent approach, at times taking over a year, where I had lost my patience. But she was confident that she would get through. I never discouraged her or even tried to intervene. The point is not to prove myself right or wrong. It is to allow her to go forward with her intuition as she believes in it, and I believe in her. Even though I don't know whether the project would work at the outset, I support her if she feels she needs additional backing for a meeting or a suggestion on drafting an email or just by sharing my ideas and opinions. Her approach towards me is also very similar. This takes our partnership bond to the next level of understanding.

Over the years, as we continue to work with each other, we have learned a lot about each other, getting familiar with how the other approaches a task, the work culture, the background, etc. Initially, her idea about my work method was that it was very firm, fixed and not flexible, and prone to making quick judgments. Today, even though my working method has remained the same, her view towards it has changed now. She comprehends better how I analyze things and why I do things the way I do them.

What I have experienced a lot of times is that business partners take working together as a challenge and, in doing so, try to show they are better, superior, comparatively and try to be dominant over the other. It is always said that two strong personalities are hard to bind to form a firm partnership. But today, I disagree with this idea. Carbon steel, the most durable and reliable metal known in the industry, can only be formed if iron and carbon are alloyed together. Similarly, **to form a partnership as strong as steel, one has to alloy with a reliable partner**. No matter how strong the iron is, without carbon, it can't have the properties of steel.

Between Nadiya and I, we have found that balance; we both have aggressive natures, as Lyndon Johnson has also seconded that "Success always feeds the appetite of aggression." However, we always respect each other's strengths, trying to complement each other and encourage each other. We have differences, disagreements, and conflicts, and that is all very understandable. We both know we are on the same side and are working toward common goals. Even though many times our discussions also turn into arguments, in the end, we share a common strength to convert this into a positive dialogue.

This is what I regard to be a true synergy between business partners. We share a broader view of things and don't get into the nitty-gritty by trying to prove to the other who is superior. Working together as one, investing, discussing, strategizing, understanding, keeping our differences apart, achieving common goals without ego, and encouraging each other with a true sense of trust and a belief that is sometimes beyond understanding is our motto. Picking each other up, accepting the mistakes of each other, and having a broad acceptance, giving each other credit, complimenting, and criticizing each other to help better the person is the secret behind our success. All of this is accomplished with good vibes and positivity.

My synopsis of the right business partner: A true partnership is like a three-legged race, holding and supporting your partner, understanding that if your partner falls, you fall with them. You can't free yourself and run to the finish line to proclaim a win. It is not about reaching the finish point alone.

Generally, people forget to understand that you and your partner are one and do not need to compete. Partnerships can help you reach a point that others struggle to reach alone. Be true, be honest, be balanced, and be fair to work together as one, with sincerity. Learn from each other's life and work experiences, enhancing and supporting the other with the right intentions, the right objectives to achieve it, and the right attitude to do so.

In the end, I would like to quote one of my idols and one of the greatest businessmen the world has known—Aristotle Onassis, who stated: "I have no friends and no enemies—only competitors." I feel this is so true and the most amazing statement made by a great achiever. But at the same time, I would like to remind people that a business partner is an ally; a business partnership is like a conjugal tie where you are not <u>a</u> part but <u>the</u> part of one another. You are always on the same side, aiming for the same goal.

A true partnership can only prevail if you think of yourself as one with your partner, energizing every move, every act, and every action as part of mutual growth. This is the practical truth behind having a successful business partnership and my perception of **Synergy: A Synopsis of an Elite Business Partnership!**

About the Authors

Nadiya is a global international trade leader with a diverse educational and professional background. She holds two Master's degrees in Business Management and Genetics, majoring in Polymorphic Genetic Markers in the Development of Breast Cancer.

Starting her career in the banking sector in Ukraine, she pursued her passion for global markets by moving to Egypt to work for an export-import trading company. Later, she relocated to the UAE, where she held prominent positions in some of the leading FMCG industry companies on the globe.

With deep insights into product development, manufacturing challenges, and technical aspects of various products, she founded INAS EXIM LLC in 2015, specializing in customized food solutions for Retail, Industrial production, and HoReCa Sectors. Nadiya has also shared her extensive international business experiences through contributions to various magazines, including Authority Magazine, CIO Times, Tycoon Success, Thrive Global, and more.

Nadiya's passion for preserving nature and her commitment to the mission of the Equal Earth project led her to participate in a Woman Empowerment competition. There, she showcased a dress made entirely from recycled paper and jute thread, making a powerful statement about sustainable fashion and waste reduction. In recognition of her efforts, she was honored with the title of Best Personality at the Women Empowerment Platform in the UAE in 2020 also, bagging an award of second runners-up in the competition.

Furthermore, Nadiya developed expertise in creating environmentally friendly wall decorations under the brand *Mystique*. Through this venture, she aims to raise awareness about pollution and environmental challenges, with a particular focus on the Equal Earth project, which aims to restore the balance between humanity and nature.

In September 2022, Nadiya published her first business book, "Synergy: A Synopsis of an Elite Business Partnership," chronicles her journey from an ordinary child in a middle-class family to a successful entrepreneur. The book explores her experiences in international trade, business management, and the values that shaped her remarkable career.

Through her multifaceted endeavors, Nadiya strives to create a lasting impact on the world by advocating for sustainable practices, promoting a harmonious relationship between humanity and nature, empowering women, and facilitating international trade.

Vinay Gandhi: A Visionary Entrepreneur Behind Golden
Star International's Success

Vinay Gandhi, the visionary owner of Golden Star International, has emerged as a prominent figure in the world of business and trade. With a deep understanding of international markets and a keen eye for lucrative opportunities, Gandhi has steered his company towards remarkable success, cementing its position as a global leader in the industry. Let's delve into the key aspects of Vinay Gandhi's journey and his role in shaping Golden Star International.

Entrepreneurial Spirit and Early Beginnings: Vinay Gandhi's entrepreneurial journey began with a strong determination to create a name for himself in the business world. Armed with an indomitable spirit and a drive to succeed, he embarked on his path by establishing Golden Star International. From its humble beginnings, the company has grown exponentially under Gandhi's leadership, reaching new heights year after year.

Global Trade Expertise: One of the standout qualities of Vinay Gandhi is his deep understanding of global trade dynamics. With an acute knowledge of various industries and markets, he has capitalized on emerging opportunities, establishing strong networks and partnerships across the globe. Gandhi's adeptness at identifying untapped markets and anticipating trends has been instrumental in the expansion of Golden Star International's reach.

Diversified Portfolio: Under Vinay Gandhi's guidance, Golden Star International has developed a diversified portfolio spanning multiple sectors. The company is involved in a wide range of industries, including import-export, trading, logistics, and distribution. By strategically diversifying its operations, Golden Star International has not only mitigated risks but also maximized its potential for growth and profitability.

Commitment to Quality and Innovation: Vinay Gandhi places great emphasis on delivering high-quality products and services. Recognizing that customer satisfaction is paramount to sustaining success, he has instilled a culture of excellence within Golden Star International. Gandhi's commitment to innovation has also played a pivotal role in keeping the company ahead of the curve. By embracing cutting-edge technologies and exploring innovative business models, he has ensured that Golden Star International remains at the forefront of industry advancements.

Corporate Social Responsibility: Beyond business success, Vinay Gandhi understands the importance of giving back to society. As a responsible corporate citizen, he has through Golden Star International supported programs to environmental conservation efforts through its partner associate company Equal Earth. Gandhi actively contributes to the betterment of communities around the world.

Future Outlook: Looking ahead, Vinay Gandhi remains focused on driving Golden Star International towards continued growth and success. With a forward-thinking approach, he aims to explore new markets, leverage emerging technologies, and forge strategic partnerships that will further elevate the company's position in the global arena. Gandhi's unwavering dedication and unwavering commitment to excellence make him a formidable force in the business landscape.

In conclusion, Vinay Gandhi, the owner of Golden Star International, is an exemplary entrepreneur who has leveraged his expertise in global trade, diversified portfolio, commitment to quality, and corporate social responsibility to propel his company to remarkable success. With his visionary leadership, Gandhi continues to steer Golden Star

International towards a bright and prosperous future, leaving an indelible mark on the business world.

"Mystique" – Sea Shell Art created with Passion, Sensibility, Innovation, Skillfulness giving a Strong message and also enhancing your life and lifestyle.

An art for Nature Lovers created by 100% recyclable, bio-degradable, ocean friendly material that not only energize your thoughts but the very fauna of each material used in it helps the surroundings to create a positive energy.

"Mystique" a unique form of art created by carefully collected selective Seashells to help enrich Beauty and Blessing of Nature. According to Feng Shui and Vaastu Seashells have its own aura and energy field that enhances positivity, inviting good vibes into our home or workplace, it is believed in Feng Shui, seas-shells come loaded with luck. Because of their association with the sea, which connects distant places, shells are supposed to enhance travel luck as well as strengthen relationships. Seashells also provide relief from stress and offer a protective shield. A symbol of good communication, positive and healthy relationships and prosperity.

Signifying the Love and Gratitude towards the Universe, Mystique - An Art beyond…!

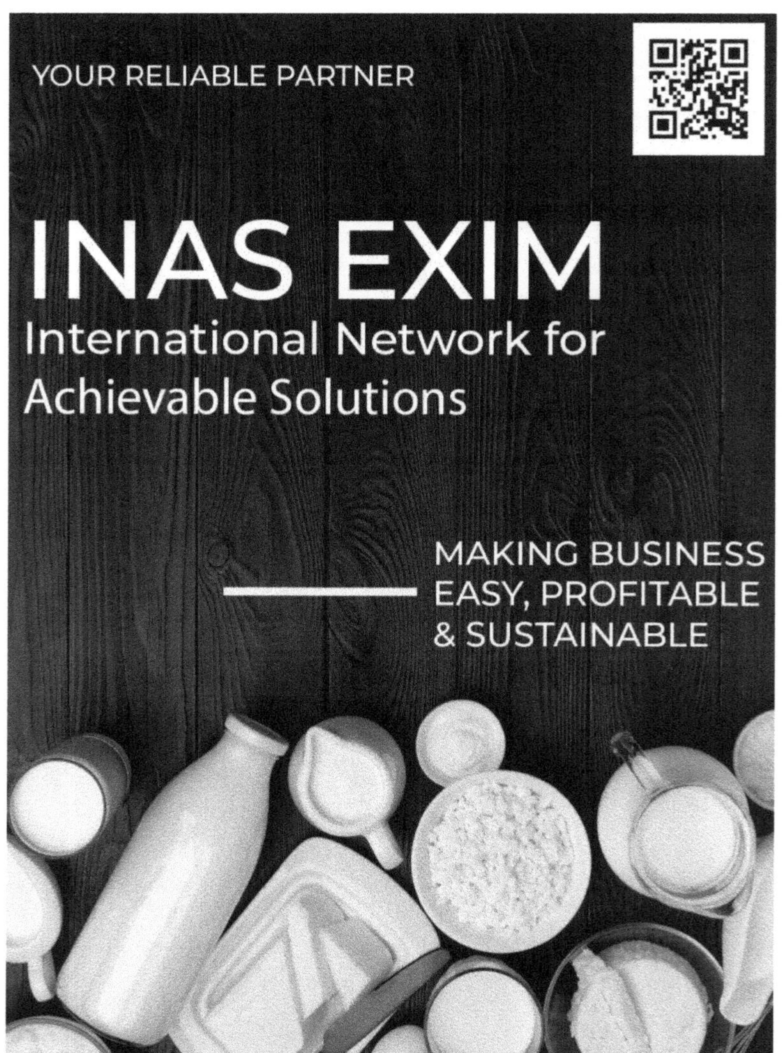
YOUR RELIABLE PARTNER
INAS EXIM
International Network for
Achievable Solutions
MAKING BUSINESS
EASY, PROFITABLE
& SUSTAINABLE

For any collaboration, connect to the authors

Nadiya Albishchenko

https://www.linkedin.com/in/nadiya-albishchenko-3474b739/

https://www.instagram.com/nadiiaalbishchenko/

https://www.facebook.com/nadiya.albishchenko/

Vinay Gandhi

https://www.linkedin.com/in/vinay-gandhi-a9650a26/

Author's website

https://thecreativeauthors.com/